'I think it would be better if you found another place to stay,' Kate said.

Jess digested the news. 'Why?'

'Because we're dangerous to each other's peace of mind. Because you're going to be here another three weeks and I'm not sure I can hold out that long.'

'No,' he said.

She glared at him in frustration.

'I'm not going to run, Kate. You're afraid of what's between us. So am I. But we're adults. We can handle it.'

'But what if, some night, we're weak at the same time?'

Following an impulse stronger than common sense, he sat beside her then laid his hand along her jaw and turned her face to his. 'Is this what you mean?'

Claiming her surprised mouth, he held the kiss to gentleness when everything in him clamoured for urgency and hot, wild sharing.

'See?' Jess said, his breath coming more rapidly. 'No problem.'

Dear Reader,

A warm welcome to Special Edition.

Considering Kate, a new STANISLASKI novel by number one *New York Times* bestselling author Nora Roberts, is our first book this month and also available from mid-July is the linked book, *The Stanislaski Sisters*, which contains Kate's mother's story.

Our popular THAT'S MY BABY! mini-series continues with *My Little One* by Linda Randall Wisdom. See how this marriage-of-convenience-for-the-sake-of-the-baby story turns out. Talking of children, look out for the first book in a new trilogy from wonderful author Laurie Paige. *Something To Talk About* begins THE WINDRAVEN LEGACY where newly-discovered secrets threaten to shatter the lives and loves of this family. The second book, *When I See Your Face*, is out in July.

The third of the MONTANA BRIDES linked books—*Just Pretending* by Myrna Mackenzie—storms onto the shelves this month. Along with five orphaned children, including nine-month-old triplets, in *Mother in a Moment* by Allison Leigh and a passionate lone wolf in *Gray Wolf's Woman* by Peggy Webb.

Enjoy!

The Editors

Something To Talk About

LAURIE PAIGE

™ SILHOUETTE®
SPECIAL EDITION™

*First published in Great Britain 2002
Silhouette Books, Eton House, 18-24 Paradise Road,
Richmond, Surrey TW9 1SR*

© Olivia M Hall 2001

ISBN 0 373 24396 0

23-0602

*Printed and bound in Spain
by Litografia Rosés S.A., Barcelona*

In loving memory, to 'Big Sis.'
You were always there for us.

LAURIE PAIGE

says, 'One of the nicest things about writing romances is researching locales, careers and ideas. In the interest of authenticity, most writers will try anything...once.' Along with her writing adventures, Laurie has been a NASA engineer, a past president of the Romance Writers of America (twice!), a mother and a grandmother (twice, also!). She was twice a Romance Writers of America RITA Award finalist for Best Traditional Romance, and has won awards from *Romantic Times Magazine* for Best Silhouette Special Edition and Best Silhouette. Recently re-settled in northern California, Laurie is looking forward to whatever experiences her next novel will send her on.

Dear Reader,

Sometimes a book is born from a sentence or phrase I hear, or the lyrics of a song. Once it was an incident I read in a magazine while sitting in the dentist's office. The Windraven Legacy was born while hiking in the Wind River region of Wyoming. After a hard climb on a trail that led up over a ridge, I stopped at the top and simply stared. Before me was a magnificent vista—deep blue sky, a mountain carved into a cirque by a glacier that had passed that way thousands of years ago, gleaming snow lying in the hollow scoured into the granite and a lake formed by the melting snow, all within a perfect postcard of a valley blooming with wildflowers and lined with pine and fir trees.

In this valley, now owned by the National Forest Service, I found an abandoned house, once part of a prosperous ranch. I sat on the porch steps and ate lunch while the wind whispered through the trees. I could almost hear the voices from the past, murmuring of love and happiness, of loss and despair. In a cottonwood along a nearby creek, a raven cawed. Another answered. Their calls were indescribably lonely. The story of the Windoms and Herriots took shape in my mind…

Laurie Paige

Chapter One

Jess Fargo parked his pickup under the cool green shadow of a live oak arching over the gravel driveway and shut off the engine. The sheer bliss of not watching the road or squinting into the hot June sun lasted about two seconds.

Then the pain in his leg kicked in.

He cursed silently and long, but words didn't ease the shower of hot needles aimed at a spot directly under his left kneecap. He willed the pain into submission.

"You want to stay here or go in?" he asked Jeremy.

"Stay here," Jeremy answered in the shorthand of youth.

His son. Ten years old. Rangy as a winter deer. Silent. Resentful. A sackcloth-and-ashes martyr to parental whims.

His ex hadn't wanted to let him see his son at all when they'd divorced five years ago. Then, two weeks ago, she shows up at the apartment, announces she's getting married again and she can't handle *his* son, so he'll have to take the boy.

Bingo! He's a full-time father again...with a shattered knee and uncertain prospects about his future.

Washed up. Has-been. He squashed the descriptive words as they seared across his brain.

Since he'd put in his twenty years and had been injured in the line of duty, he would have a pension from the Houston PD, so all was not lost.

Wasn't life just too damn wonderful? Jess thought as he climbed down from the truck.

Standing on the springy grass, the dappled, afternoon light shifting in soft patterns across the green, he studied the house and gardens.

His years as a cop had taught him to ask another cop when he needed information. The house was precisely as described by the police detective in Wind River, Wyoming, where he'd stopped to inquire about a place to stay. Its location couldn't be better for his purposes.

The yellow Victorian had black shutters and white trim. Its posts and spindles were graceful but sturdy. A porch, with a white wooden swing hanging from its rafters, wrapped across the front and disappeared around the side of the building.

The house, the valley, the snow-tipped mountain peaks poking at the sky—the whole area looked like the set for one of those ideal-family TV shows where the major sin was using someone else's hairbrush without asking. On "mean street," as cops called the ones where violence reigned, *that* could get a person diced into salad-size bits real quick.

A bitterness that had nothing to do with the post-card prettiness of the scene and everything to do with home and family and his own expectations of life rose in him.

He turned, wanting only to get out of there, then sucked air between his teeth as agony lashed at his leg. God, he hated being weak. He clutched the door handle of the pickup until the pain receded. When he could think clearly again, he acknowledged he needed a resting place. That's why he was here.

The garage was nestled in the shade of two walnut trees, the door open, disclosing a beige four-door compact station wagon. It was the type of car a woman living alone would drive—dependable, not too big, but capable of carrying a rosebush home from a nursery or hauling boxes of clothing to the church bazaar, exactly the vehicle he'd have picked for Kate Mulholland, a "wonderful, but reclusive widow," according to the detective.

The widow also had an apartment over the garage. Two bedrooms. Private. Away from noise and traffic and people. Perfect. His other reasons for choosing this locale, besides rest and recuperation, made it ideal.

But first things first. He'd better find the widow and see about the apartment. Just as he reached into the truck for his cane, a scream rent the air. He instinctively crouched.

Dropping the cane and grabbing his gun instead, he muttered, "Stay down," to his son and headed around the side of the house at a fast hobble. And came to a dead stop.

The woman shrieked again as the garden hose, loose and writhing around on the grass like some kind of demented green snake, slung a stream of water over her face and chest. The stream hit the back steps of the house, slid across the kitchen windows, slapped him in the face and slithered back the other way, covering the same objects on the return trip.

Cursing, Jess looked around for the tap. However, the widow beat him to it. While he'd been getting his drenching, she'd run to the faucet. With several deft turns she had the monster subdued in a limp coil on the ground between them.

In the silence he saw a hundred things at once. The way her dark hair gleamed with fiery sparks in the late-afternoon sun. The transparency of her wet T-shirt and the bra that was clearly visible beneath it. The dark nipples of her breasts, beaded from the cold water. The drip of water down her faded slacks, which clung damply to her hips and long legs. The way her bare toes, with bright red nails crinkled as she pressed them into the serpentine green of the grass, as if she were embarrassed at being bested by the marauding hose.

Also, the dart of fear across her face as she faced him.

Her eyes, big and blue and truly beautiful, gleamed in the sunlight. Other emotions mixed with the fear and flitted briefly through their depths.

Slowly she raised her hands. "Don't shoot," she said, a hint of careful humor mixed with the wariness. "We'll go peacefully." With her foot she jabbed the hose as if it were her companion in crime. Her voice was pure honey.

The words hit home. He glanced at the gun with a scowl, then shoved it into the back waistband of his jeans. He couldn't take his eyes off her. There was something real and urgent and compelling about her...and something elusive and mystical. He couldn't explain it.

"Sorry. I thought you were being attacked," he said, his tone harsh as he tried to close the breach in his emotional defenses with the anger that usually drowned out all else.

She gestured in apology. "You got wet—"

"It's okay, Kate. Don't fuss."

She visibly drew back, her gaze suspicious. "How do you know my name? I don't know you." She picked up the garden rake.

"Detective Bannock sent me. She told me your name, what you looked like." He spoke curtly, like a cop on a case. He tried to keep his eyes above her neckline. He cursed again. That didn't erase the picture of her from his inner vision, though, or cool the blood that pounded hotly through him.

The last thing he needed was a fractious libido to go with his other problems. He glanced down at his soaked shirt.

Washed up. Has-been.

"Shannon sent you?" the widow asked.

"Yeah, she said you had an apartment I could rent. I'm Jess Fargo, Houston Police Department. I'll show you my ID." He reached slowly into his hip pocket for his wallet.

The water and the breeze produced a cooling effect.

He could see goose bumps on her arms and neck. Her nipples were still tight. A shudder ran through him, reminding him of all the things he had once liked about a warm and willing woman. Well, he still liked some things…except the closeness sex demanded and the emotional baggage women wanted as a result.

He flipped open his wallet and held the badge toward her. When she didn't move, he took a step. His left knee buckled.

Flinging out a hand for balance as he teetered awkwardly, he encountered the rake, then warm flesh. An arm wrapped around his waist. She dropped the rake and took part of his weight until he got his legs under him again.

"Are you okay?" she asked. "Did you hurt your leg?"

"Got it shot up during an arrest last month. It isn't real stable just yet." He gritted the words as pain raced up his thigh and lodged in his spine.

"Oh, that's too bad." Her sympathy was real and immediate.

He directed an irritated glance her way, then lingered, fascinated by the fine hairs at her temples, each glowing like a dark ember as the wind tumbled them in the sunlight.

"You smell good," he said, the words springing from a need inside him that he hadn't known existed.

"Lemon basil, I suspect. I've been weeding it." She glanced over her shoulder. "Can you get up the steps? Or I'll bring you a chair—"

"I'll manage. Just let me hold on to you."

"Of course."

She was compassionate but brisk, and he was pretty

sure she didn't know about the wet T-shirt. Or what it was doing to him. If so, she had more guile than any woman he'd ever met.

"Lean on me as much as you need," she invited while she eyed the distance to the house and obviously appraised their chances of getting there. "I'm pretty strong."

She was. Beneath the curves, he could feel the ripple of toned muscles as she tried to take more of his weight. He held on with an arm about her shoulders, aware of one firm breast snug against his cracked rib, which had gotten its share of punishment in the shootout and ensuing tussle.

Her hold hurt yet felt so unbearably good he would have begged her to continue even knowing his rib was going to puncture his heart if she did.

He was startled at the admission. He hadn't realized he needed contact with another human this badly—

"Are you sure you're okay?"

He stared into eyes so pure a blue they defined the color. "Your eyes," he murmured, trying to find words for them.

She lowered the naturally dark lashes with their enticing curl at the ends, shielding her eyes from his gaze. "You'll get used to them," she said in an offhand manner. "Are you ready?"

"Yes."

A groan forced its way between his clenched lips as he put weight on his throbbing knee. The run, then the sudden stop and his full weight coming down on the rebuilt bone and the synthetic replacement kneecap had probably undone a month's worth of healing.

He cursed silently, the sensual hunger at last beaten into submission by the pain of movement.

A cynical wisdom murmured that her guilt over his pain might be the best way into the apartment over the garage. He stumbled a bit as they struggled up the short set of stairs and wasn't sure if it was deliberate or due to the weakness in his leg. She tightened her grip and cast him a worried glance as they eased into the house.

"There," the widow said, lowering her arms to let him settle on a comfortable maple kitchen chair.

He didn't let his arm trail across her back or hips as they disengaged, but he had a sudden, surprising sensation about how it might feel. Clenching his teeth, he tried to overcome the thoughts that stabbed at him as relentlessly as the hot needles in his leg.

"Would you like a glass of tea?" she asked.

"You have anything stronger?"

"Bourbon."

"A double." He wiped water and the sweat of painful effort off his face with a hand that shook. "Nothing like being as weak as a baby in front of a woman."

He tried to smile in order to wipe the concern out of her eyes. Pity was the one thing he didn't need and wouldn't accept from anyone.

"That's okay. Shall I fix an ice bag for your knee?"

"No, it'll be okay." He laid his gun on a pink-and-green-striped place mat on the table and leaned back with a bone-weary sigh against a cushion tied to the chair.

A chintz-and-china type, he decided, glancing

around the spotless kitchen with its bright floral touches. Down-to-earth, too. She had the soft Western drawl he'd noticed in the female police detective. It was pleasant—

"Dad?"

Jess jerked around with a frown. Jeremy stood with his nose an inch from the screen door, gazing in at them.

"I thought I told you to stay in the truck," he said, the sharp edge of his anger and pain boiling over.

The widow gave him a puzzled frown, then turned a dazzling smile toward the door. "Hi, come on in. It's open."

Jeremy stood on the step, his bony kid's face set in a mulish scowl, and stared at him through the screen. Jess tamped down his temper. "You heard the lady. Come in."

The boy slid inside and stood a foot from the door like a wild creature staying near his escape hole.

Jess felt the regret rise all at once, bitter with his own resentment in acknowledgment of lost opportunities with this person who was a carbon copy of his younger, once idealistic self. Pain hit him again, this time in his heart. No one had ever told him regret was so hard to live with.

His gaze collided with the woman's. Her incredible eyes filled with pity. The cold shield of past humiliations snapped shut around him. He might be a has-been cop, but at least he wasn't a falling-down drunk the way his own father had been. Saturday-night brawls had been the order of life in his youth. His son had never had to face that. The boy had had it easy compared to the neighborhood where he'd grown up.

He shook off the memories of the past and concentrated on the pain of the present. He struggled to pull the jeans leg up, but it was hopeless. The material was too tight, his knee too swollen.

"I'll help, Dad. You'd better get some ice on that. Remember what the doctor said."

Jess was surprised at his son's concern, then doubly so when Jeremy dropped to his haunches in front of him and tried to help. "It's okay, son. I'll take care of it later."

He glanced up to find his hostess observing him with a slight frown line between her eyes. A sense of her uneasiness came to him. "You'll need an ice pack," she said, and set to work with an unnecessary show of industry.

He hesitated, then retrieved a knife from his pocket and proceeded to split the jeans along the seam. The scar tissue, when exposed, was an angry red welt along the top and side of his knee. The flesh puffed out like an adder about to strike. So much for taking it easy for three months.

"Damn," he said softly.

She turned to face him and dropped the container of ice she'd removed from the freezer. Ice cubes hit and skittered across the shining green-and-white kitchen floor.

"Oh, shoot," she said in aggrieved tones, not looking his way. She scooped some cubes into a plastic bag, added some water and zipped it closed. Her face was pale.

"Sorry, I didn't mean to startle you."

He was puzzled at the tremor in her hand when she handed the bag to him. He saw her glance at his knee, then away. It was the scars that bothered her. Funny, but he wouldn't have taken her for the squeamish sort.

While he placed the ice pack on his leg, she swept the icy debris out the back door. None of the wary humor he'd noticed earlier was visible. What was it with a woman who could face down a stranger with a gun but was profoundly disturbed at the sight of a few scars?

A woman who had been terribly frightened by something in her past, the cop in him answered. He hated it when women and children were hurt, often by the very men who were supposed to look after and protect them. Which was why he'd become a cop, he supposed.

"I won't hurt you," he said in the same soothing tone he used with victims of domestic violence, the same tone she'd used with him while facing his weapon.

"Of course not. I never thought you would." She replaced the broom in the closet. Her eyes met his for a second.

The sparkle was back, and he breathed deeply as the tension in his stomach uncoiled. "The ice is helping. The swelling seems to have stopped, and the pain is easing up."

"Good." She poured a double shot of bourbon and set the glass on the place mat near the gun. "Would you excuse me? I need to change clothes."

"Sure. We'll be here." He wasn't going anywhere fast on that knee.

She smiled and nodded, then hurried out. He heard her footsteps on the stairs a second later.

Kate locked her bedroom door and dashed to the bedside phone. She called the number that went straight to Shannon's line at the police department.

"Bannock, here."

"Shannon—"

"Hi, Kate. No, I have not forgotten your birthday luncheon tomorrow. I even got you a card."

"I'm expecting homemade cookies, too. Lots of 'em."

"Oh, all right," Shannon replied with pretend grumpiness.

"Shannon, did you send a policeman out to my place? A guy by the name of..." She couldn't remember.

"Jess Fargo. Yeah. He needs a place to recuperate from an injury, wants to fish and relax in the country with his son, he said. I take it they arrived safely?"

Kate thought of the hose and the gun. "Well, yes. I just wanted to follow up on his credentials. I hadn't planned on renting the apartment now that Valerie has married and moved out. I thought I'd have the summer to myself."

Val, a local elementary school teacher, had snagged the only eligible doctor in town, much to several other citiziens' chagrin. She and the doctor were on their honeymoon.

'You're turning into a hermit," her cousin teased before turning serious once more. "About the cop. He really needs a place. He's been driving for a couple of days and realized he was getting too tired to continue. He thought the fishing might be good around here.''

''Okay, that checks out. Thanks. I guess only a black-hearted witch would throw out an injured officer of the law.''

''Right. He's handsome in a sort of world-weary, seen-it-all manner, huh?''

Kate heard the laughter in Shannon's voice. ''He's cynical and probably hard-hearted. Talk to you later,'' she promised and hung up. She headed for the shower.

The sight that greeted her in the full-length mirror on the door caused her to gasp and throw her arms across her chest in shock.

Even as she made the gesture, she realized the futility of it. Jess Fargo, and his son, had already seen her. Slowly she released the hold she had across her chest and sighed in dismay at the near transparency of her shirt and bra. Even her nipples were visible as two distinct dark pebbles under the wet cloth.

She sank down on the bed and pressed her hands over her face. The detective would think…he must think the worst.

But it wasn't as if she had exposed herself on purpose. She hadn't known he was coming.

Kate stood and muttered an expletive. She had spent eighteen months in therapy after her husband's death, trying to get over the sense of shame he had forced onto her. If she so much as glanced at another man or spoke to a male friend, he'd accused her of vile acts—

No! She wouldn't go back to that time and those

feelings of helplessness and despair. She was not at fault here.

After taking a quick shower, she dressed in a broadcloth shirt, leaving the tails untucked, and blue slacks with an elastic waist. She pulled her damp hair through a stretchy band and secured it at the base of her neck. With pink lip gloss and a pair of white sandals she was ready.

Taking a calming breath, she marched down the steps. It wasn't her fault, she repeated on the way, her mantra during the days, weeks, months, after Kris's death.

Jess Fargo was where she had left him. That was a relief. She liked people who did as expected. His son had again taken up a position near the door. She felt the underlying tension between the father and son as her eyes met those of the boy.

It was like looking into her own soul. She recognized the resentment, the need to be *wanted* and, with it, the hope that still lingered in his young and bruised heart. Pain stitched through her in painful jabs even as she looked away and told herself she was imagining things.

Sympathy rose in her. The youngster needed something more from the man, perhaps more visible signs of his father's love.

No! It wasn't her business. She wouldn't get sucked into their problems. She had found contentment. She wanted only to be left in peace. But she hated to see the boy so lost and unsure and resentful.

She sighed. There she went again—Kate, the tenderhearted, caretaker to wounded dogs, cats, humans.

Her throat closed. She had to swallow a couple of

times before she could talk. "I spoke to my cousin, the police detective. She says you need a place to stay for a few days."

"Yeah. Maybe a month."

She frowned, then shrugged. A month wasn't so long that their lives would become entangled. "There's an apartment over the garage. You'll want to see it first—"

"It'll be fine."

His interruption told her he didn't care what it looked like. He needed a place to rest. Sympathy stirred again.

Jess Fargo's problems were his own, she reminded herself sternly. Maybe this trip would work for him and his son, maybe not. She would keep her nose out of their troubles.

"I didn't catch your name," she said to the boy.

"Jeremy Fargo."

"You in high school yet?" she asked. Actually, he looked to be about eleven, maybe twelve.

His smile was quick and shy and pleased. "I'll be in sixth grade this fall."

"He's tall for his age," his father put in. She watched him adjust the ice pack on his knee, then take a sip of iced tea after a glance at the empty bourbon glass.

Kate didn't offer him more. She figured he'd had a medicinal dose and that was enough.

The words were on the tip of her tongue to invite them to dinner, though. She doubted the tough cop had shopped for groceries, and the ranch was a long way from Wind River and even farther from Medicine Bow, where a larger supermarket was located. She suppressed the invitation, knowing instinctively that this man was dangerous to her peace of mind. Hadn't she learned anything from her marriage?

The memory of other summers flooded her heart with the bitter sadness of loss. It was a pain that never seemed to diminish but lingered always at the edges of her emotions, ready to catch her at moments of weakness.

Such as when she'd seen the scars on the detective's knee.

Gunshot wounds. She knew them well. She knew the terror, the pain that tore through the flesh, and with it the knowledge that she had lost something more precious than her own life. She laid a hand over her abdomen where another heart had once beat with the quick expectancy of the very young.

Her child. Her son that would never be.

The emptiness rose like bile to her throat. Her arms, her heart, her home—empty of that sweet life that should have been.

Dear God, she silently pleaded, seeking relief from that terrible, terrible memory. She couldn't go back to thinking about what might have been. With control learned at a price, she forced her thoughts to the guests in her kitchen.

Like Jess Fargo, there were scars on her flesh, but they didn't compare to the ones in her soul.

"Come," she said, standing abruptly, "I'll take you to the apartment and let you get settled in."

"I'll get your cane, Dad," Jeremy volunteered. He ran out, leaving a wake of silence behind him.

He was back in less than a minute. She headed out

the door, leaving father and son to follow at their own pace.

Coolness eddied around her when she opened the door to the apartment. She turned on the refrigerator and hot water heater. After opening the sliding glass doors on to the deck over the garage, she stood there, letting the breeze blow over her as she gazed at the peaceful scene.

The deck commanded a wonderful view of the stock lake to the south of them, where cattle had gathered for an afternoon drink, and of snow-tipped Medicine Bow Peak to the southwest of them. Walnut trees shaded the area from the afternoon sun.

Hearing the hesitant step and the thump of the cane on the stairs, Kate again felt a tug of pity. The handsome, brooding Jess Fargo would once have bounded up those steps two at a time with the ease of a mountain elk.

Turning from the view, she noted the brief clenching of his teeth as he maneuvered up the final step and across the threshold, his grip on the cane evident. She wondered if he would ever move easily and swiftly again.

He paused, taking in everything about the apartment—the roomy kitchen, the living room through an archway, the homey furniture that had been handed down for generations.

There were also two bedrooms down a short hallway. The bathroom was tucked under the eaves at the end of the hall.

''It's small,'' she said, feeling a need to apologize.

''It'll do.'' He pulled out a chair and sat at the pine

table that had belonged to her great-grandmother, his legs extended out in front of him.

"There are dishes, but I'll have to bring you towels and linens—"

"We have sleeping bags and towels," he cut in.

His lips were crimped at the corners, indicating pain or anger or both. She hadn't thought about the difficulty of the steps for an injured person until he'd had to climb them.

"There's a motel closer to town that's reasonable in price. You wouldn't have to go up and down steps."

"I can handle the steps," he informed her.

She recoiled from the bitter anger that flashed in his eyes, eyes that were the color of shadowed oak leaves, their muted green rimmed with a dark circle of gray.

"Then I'll leave you to get settled. My number is on the pad beside the wall phone. Call if you need anything."

"A key," he said.

She was puzzled briefly, then she smiled tightly. "It's on the hook by the phone. Folks rarely lock up around here."

"That's foolish. It can even be deadly. You don't know who might come around."

The disgust of the professional crime fighter at the willful stupidity of people grated over her nerves.

"Well, now that I have a police officer on the premises, I'm sure I'll be safe."

She flicked a glance at the son and was sorry for the tone she'd used. The boy was watching them warily, a young creature caught between two larger, opposing forces. As he'd probably been between his parents. Just a hunch, but Kate was pretty sure the parents were divorced. No wife had been mentioned.

"The fish start biting at first light," she told him with a real smile. "The path to the lake starts at the end of the garden. Just go through the rose trellis and follow the trail. There's a pier. Feel free to use it. Fishing poles are in the garden shed near the roses."

"Thanks," Jeremy said politely.

She left them to their own devices. Later that evening, sitting on the swing, she observed the light in the windows over the garage. Jeremy and his father had made several trips to the pickup truck with the camper shell. Foolish man, to torture his leg that way. She and Jeremy could have managed to bring everything up on their own.

Pride. Stubbornness. A chip on his shoulder. He was a man who needed to come to terms with life, a man who needed to reach out to his son, who had his own unfulfilled needs.

Foreboding rippled through her. A wise woman would stay out of the way of both father and son.

Chapter Two

But when had women ever been wise when it came to growing boys who, in their eyes, needed nurturing? Kate chided herself as she carried a basket of hot muffins and just-picked strawberries up the steps to the apartment. She had a mug of coffee and a pitcher of milk with her.

The door to the apartment was open when she arrived at the landing. Jess stood there, his face expressionless, but she sensed the scowl.

"I brought Jeremy some hot muffins," she said.

A flicker of suspicion darted through his eyes, then was gone, replaced by an implacable wall of distrust that made her angry. He had levied a judgment against her for no reason, and she didn't like it.

After an eternity he opened the screen door and let her in. "He isn't up yet," her new tenant informed her.

The scent of his aftershave stroked her senses. He was apparently just out of the shower, his dark hair still damp, his face smooth from a shave. He seemed as fresh as the crisp morning air that cascaded down from the lofty peaks overlooking the long, broad valley. The strain she'd noticed yesterday had eased somewhat from around his eyes. He looked rested, although not completely restored, and she realized how tired he must have been when he and his son had arrived.

Against her will, pity stirred as she stepped past him into the apartment. He had been injured in the line of duty and asked for nothing except a place to recuperate—and maybe a chance to reestablish a closeness with his son.

He wore a T-shirt and khaki shorts. His feet were bare. The bruises, the scars, the tightly stretched skin, all told of unremitting pain that had to be endured because there was no other way. The crimped lines at the corners of his mouth spoke louder than his fierce denial of need.

It was a thing she'd done for months on end—this holding back, this keeping within, all the misery that cried out from the depths of a person. She knew about things like that. Suddenly the tears were close to the surface.

Drawn against her will into a maelstrom of past emotion that she didn't want or need, she crossed swiftly to the table and set the feast down. "I'll just leave everything. I brought some milk."

He made a sound that could have been a mumble of gratitude. She put the container of milk in the refrigerator. On the counter was a spoon and a jar of instant coffee.

"There's fresh-brewed coffee, too." She put the insulated mug on the counter beside the spoon.

"Thanks." He waited by the door for her to leave.

The return path took her past him. Nervousness made her clumsy. She caught her sandal on the hooked rug in front of the door, causing a stumble. His arms were there to catch her in an instant, so fast that it took her completely by surprise.

The morning changed. First there had been the cold breeze, nipping into the apartment from the open door, then there was warmth all around her, like the sun enfolding her.

His hands spread heat into her arm and waist where he touched her. Through her slacks she felt the weight of his thigh pressed between hers, sending shafts of sunlight splintering through her abdomen. Her breath caught.

In the wary silence between them, she heard the sibilant hiss of air as he took a deep breath. She experienced the unexpected thundering of his heart. Unbidden yearning rushed through her, a flash point of need so powerful it left her helpless and subdued.

For the space of two heartbeats, she lingered in the embrace, unable to move. His pupils widened as his gaze locked with hers. The same terrible need blazed in him as in her.

Something inside leaped, startled as a young deer, then dipped crazily before righting itself.

They moved at the same time, drawing back, pulling away, dropping their arms, removing their hands from contact with hot, suddenly yearning flesh. The withdrawal signaled loss that she couldn't comprehend.

He cursed under his breath.

She sighed with relief.

"Thanks for the food," he said stiffly.

"No problem," she replied. She fled down the steps.

"What's this I hear about a good-looking stranger at your place?" Megan gave Kate a mock-severe stare, then spoiled it by grinning at Shannon.

Both Megan and Shannon were cousins to Kate from her mother's side of the family. She and Megan lived on Windraven, the family ranch once managed by their grandfather. Megan lived in the big house with their grandfather, Patrick Windom, who had suffered a stroke a few years ago. Their grandfather was in a wheelchair and had rarely spoken since his son, Megan's father, had died in an auto accident ten years ago.

"Don't ask me," Kate replied. "Shannon was the one who sent him and his son my way."

"No wife?" Megan asked.

"Not that I've seen."

"Ah," Megan said in understanding.

"He's divorced. Look, I just tried to do a favor for a fellow officer," Shannon defended herself. "When I checked him out, the sergeant in Houston told me Jess Fargo was a hero and that he'd been shot in the line of duty, protecting an innocent bystander in the street where the shoot-out occurred. His kneecap was shattered by a bullet, and even then he managed to stop the guy from taking a woman waiting at a bus stop as a hostage. Oh, and his ex is getting married again and dumped the son on him a couple of weeks ago.''

''He has scars,'' Kate said, seeing the uneven pattern of the gun wound, the neat medical incisions and the crosshatched pattern of stitches. She laid a hand over her abdomen as a sharp echo of past pain flashed through her again.

Shannon's brow crinkled in worry. ''I'm sorry, Katie, I didn't mean to make you remember.''

''You didn't. I'm okay.'' Kate summoned a smile. ''And, as usual, I felt sorry for him and his son and let them have the apartment. I'm such a sucker for a sad story.''

Remembering how she and Jess had really met, she started laughing, a little shakily but with true mirth.

''It must have been a real tear jerker,'' Megan said in a wry tone. ''Do tell all.''

Her cousins thought her story about tossing the hose down only to have the shut-off lever hit the ground and stick in the open position, then the man showing up with a gun, looking ready to shoot anything that crossed his path and also getting drenched, was hilarious.

''A great beginning,'' Shannon said, beaming at Kate. ''I predict even greater things to come.''

''Huh,'' was Kate's reaction to that.

What a trio the cousins were, Kate mused as she read absurd birthday cards and opened lovely presents—a chemise top with a lace blouse to wear over it, shorts and a shirt to go with the other two pieces, and the promised bag of cookies.

Shannon's parents had divorced when she was a

kid, so she tended to herd people into family units, although she seemed leery of matrimony for herself. Megan had had to deal with the tragedy of her mother's strange and unhappy death from drowning, plus the quarrels between her father and grandfather, then her grandfather's stroke after her uncle Sean's accident. Megan wanted everyone to get along and be happy.

Kate considered her own emotional baggage. She had always had a need to heal every wounded creature she met. Life, the very act of living, could be so very complicated and serious. Her husband had accused her of having a God complex.

She had tried to help him, to bring the joy of living back into his life, but she had failed. No, it was wrong to think that way! He had chosen his path. She had chosen to live. But she had lost their child and the ability to have more.

She'd also lost something of her faith in life, she acknowledged with a familiar stab of sadness and remorse. She could forgive Kris for shooting her, then himself, but she would never forgive the loss of the baby she'd carried for seven precious months—

"What?" she said, jolted from the past by a nudge.

"I have to get back to work," Shannon reminded them. "Some people don't have the luxury of doing what they want, when they want. Some of us hold down a real job."

"You love it," Megan declared. "You'd have to, to work in the domestic crisis unit for as long as you have."

Shannon laughed, tossed her share of the bill on the table and headed out with a wave.

"Thanks for lunch and the presents," Kate called after her. "Lunch and presents, too," she said to Megan as the waitress refilled their tea glasses. "I hope you didn't blow the budget."

"I used my own funds," Megan informed her. "I'm training three other colts along with Wind Dancer."

"Mmm, you'll probably want a raise. I think we could swing one, a small one," Kate quickly added.

As bookkeeper for the five-thousand-acre ranch, she knew to the penny what everything cost. Keeping the place going was the goal of the three cousins. After Megan's father had died in the auto accident and their grandfather had had a stroke immediately after the funeral, the three cousins, the last of their family, had banded together and determined to keep the ranch going. It hadn't been easy.

Megan shook her head, her bright coppery curls bouncing with each movement. "I'm fine. With the policeman there, you'll have income from the apartment. That will help you out."

Kate realized she'd forgotten to mention rent to her new tenant. She wondered how much he could afford. "Yes. Every dollar counts, since the price of beef dropped."

"Wouldn't it be nice if he spent the summer? Then you can get another teacher in there when school starts."

"He's only going to stay a few days, a month at the most."

"That's too bad."

Kate wasn't sure about that. "I have to run. I'm helping Rory set up his bookkeeping system."

"Have fun." Megan wrinkled her nose.

Bookkeeping was not Kate's cousin's idea of entertainment, but Kate liked it. She liked the order of numbers and the certainty of the balance sheet. She wondered if she liked those things because life had never seemed to add up, not to her. For instance, when did the good balance the bad? Shaking off the useless nostalgia, she stood. "Thanks again for the gifts."

Kate stored her presents in the car, then drove over to the offices of Dr. Rory Daniels. Kate had known Rory all her life. After finishing veterinarian training, he had gone into partnership with Doc Bloom. He was an excellent vet and an expert on horses, advising Megan on the ranch breeding program.

Tall, racehorse trim, a year behind her in age, he had coal-black hair and light-blue eyes. While she explained the bookkeeping entries on the new computer system to him and his secretary, she noticed how handsome he was...but she kept seeing Jess Fargo....

When Kate returned home in the late afternoon, she found the coffee mug and milk pitcher on her back steps, along with a check for a month's rent for the same amount she'd charged the teacher. He must have asked Shannon the rental price.

From her upstairs bedroom she could see Jeremy at the lake, sitting on the pier and staring into the water, looking forlorn. After changing clothes, she dug up some fishing worms and headed for the path to the lake with two poles.

"Hi," she called out before stepping on the rough planks.

The boy's head snapped around. For a moment she saw his misery, then the shy grin appeared. Her heart clenched in pity. Kids were hurt the most when a marriage failed.

He probably felt left out now that his mom had decided to remarry and had packed him off to his father.

"You from Houston, too?" she asked.

"Yeah."

"Going to be a cop?"

He cast her a startled glance, then shrugged.

"I thought my cousin was loony when she went into police work, but she seems to like it and she's good. The world needs people like that. Is your dad a good cop?"

Jeremy appeared shocked that she would ask. "The best," he told her. "He got a medal from the mayor for saving a woman's life even after he was shot."

She nodded. The son's pride in his dad and his admiration for the man were obvious. There was respect, too. That was good, but the youngster was lonely. His eyes, the same shadowy green as his father's held emotion too deep for one so young. He'd seen a lot of life, this kid who tugged at her heart. She sighed and looked away.

The relationship between the father and son was none of her business, she reminded herself. Stay out of it.

But there was one other thing she wanted to say to her young guest. "My mother died when I was a senior in high school. When my dad remarried a couple of years later, I resented it. I thought it was somehow a betrayal of my mother, but I realized that life goes on, you know?''

Jeremy ducked his head and studied the water lapping against the posts of the pier. He nodded jerkily.

"I felt left out of their happiness. It was kind of hard until I got used to the idea. I was sort of lost and lonely."

"My mom's boyfriend doesn't want me around," he blurted out, his voice breaking on an upward note of distress.

"Hmm." She waited a long minute. "He probably thinks the same about you—that you don't want him around. Maybe he's worried that she loves you more than she loves him. People are like that, you know, sort of insecure about things."

A frown, very like his father's, appeared on the smooth brow of the youngster. She figured she had given him enough to digest for now. Besides, she didn't want to get involved with anyone else's problems, especially those of a hardheaded detective who would be out of her life in a few weeks.

"I dug up some worms," she mentioned casually, picking up one of the rods. "I have an extra spinning outfit."

She put a worm on the hook and cast into the lake. Hardly a minute went by before she had a bite. "Bluegills. They get hungry about this time of day."

Jeremy watched her catch a fish before he picked up the rod and tried his luck. He lost a half dozen worms before he caught on. When he brought his first fish in and removed it from the hook, she saw a different person, one who was laughing and excited and happy, the way a youngster his age should be.

"Hey, that's a big one, a seven- or eight-incher. I think we'll have fresh fish for supper tonight."

The sober expression returned. "I don't know if my dad knows how to cook fish."

"No reason for him to have to. A person should be able to cook his own catch, my dad always said. We'll fry 'em up at my place and invite your father to join us. Okay?"

His grin was huge. She saw the father reflected in the son, when Jess Fargo had been young and idealistic and enthusiastic about life. A sense of sorrow overcame her. She shook it off. Jess Fargo wasn't her problem.

"Yes, ma'am," Jeremy said. "Yeah, that would be great."

"I'm Kate to my friends."

No matter what she told herself for the next hour, she knew she was being pulled in like the fish on the end of her line. But there was a kid involved, and where kids were concerned, well, she couldn't help but worry. So maybe she and Jeremy could be friends while he was there.

She counted the fish on their stringer. "We have enough. Let's clean them."

The boy followed as she led the way back to the garden and the compost heap. She removed a knife from her pocket and, on a big flat rock, cleaned her share of the catch, tossing the fish heads into a hole she dug at the edge of the compost. When she handed the knife to him, he followed her example.

At the house she dipped her fish into egg beaten

with milk, then into cornmeal. While he got his share ready, she fried her catch in oil, then let him do the same.

"You want to invite your dad to join us?" she asked when she had fries and a salad ready to go with the fish.

Jeremy looked doubtful. "He was taking a nap when I went down to the lake. I think his leg was hurting awfully bad. He took two pain killers, then went to sleep on the sofa."

"Shall I get him while you set the table under the oak tree?" She pointed at the picnic table through the window.

"Sure."

"Paper plates are in here, forks in this drawer." She pointed them out, then left, feeling quite irritated with the tough cop who didn't want anything from anyone.

She marched up the steps and knocked sharply on the door frame. Through the screen, she could see Jess's reclining form on the sofa. The television was on, the sound low.

He sat up abruptly, then swore as he swung his legs to the floor and put a hand on his injured knee.

"Supper," she called out, keeping her tone cheerful.

"What?" He glared toward the door.

"Jeremy and I caught some bluegills. They're ready to eat. At the picnic table," she added, then hurried down the steps and back to her house.

"Is Dad coming?" Jeremy asked when she joined him.

"He'll be along in a minute. He was still asleep. I

had to wake him up.'' She prepared glasses of raspberry iced tea. Handing one to Jeremy, she carried the other two outside.

She and Jeremy were seated when Jess came out of the apartment and limped down the steps with the aid of the cane. She pretended not to see his scowl. ''Come and get it,'' she advised, ''before they get cold. We each get three.''

''Kate caught five and I caught four,'' Jeremy told his father, surprising her with the use of her name.

Jess stood at the end of the table, taking in the food, then his son's somewhat defiant expression. His hostess was busily spooning salad into a bowl. She didn't glance his way. Which irritated the hell out of him.

Logic told him she had simply offered his son a chance to fish, then had let the kid enjoy the fruits of his labor. That's what logic told him. His feelings were something else.

He was angry, as if she had entered into some conspiracy to win his son away from him. Guilt ate at him. He should have taken the boy fishing instead of going to sleep. The widow was probably trying to do a good deed for a lonely kid. He wished she would leave them the hell alone.

Her eyes became guarded when he took a seat next to his son, across the wooden table from her. He realized something of his feelings must have shown in his eyes. He forced a smile on his face and heartiness into his voice.

''Now this is what I call a real meal. You two caught these in the lake in—'' He glanced at this watch ''—couldn't have taken more than an hour or so.''

"That's right, Dad. You shoulda come down. The fish were really biting. I caught two with the same worm."

Looking at Jeremy's eager face, Jess felt the familiar twist of regret. He'd neglected his son since the divorce. It had been easier to stay away than fight with the boy's mother over every single thing.

Excuses were a poor substitute for fathering, his conscience brusquely reminded him. Glancing up, he stared into eyes that were bluer than the summer sky. She saw too much, this reclusive widow who took the time to show a kid how to catch their supper. He bit back a curse at life's complications, then helped himself to fish and fries.

"Here, Jeremy. This is the big one you brought in. You get to have him," Kate said.

Their hostess forked the serving onto his son's plate with an easy manner that implied a friendship was already established between the two.

He wondered how friendly she'd feel if she discovered he was there to investigate her family. One thing she didn't know—her aunt, Megan's mother, had been his sister. Half sister, actually.

Bunny and he had shared the same mother, but different fathers. His had been the drunk, hers the nice guy. But the good die young, and Bunny's dad had died. Their mom had married his father a year later. His old man had been a loser.

Bunny had left home as soon as she got out of high school. She'd never returned. He didn't blame her for that.

For the first year after her departure, he'd been so lonely he'd thought he would die. He'd loved her more than anyone. Later, he'd realized his big sis had been the one who had raised him. She'd sung songs and told him stories. Before she left, she had told him she would always love him better than anyone in the whole world. He'd lived on that love for years after his mom had died.

One thing—he'd always had doubts about that drowning accident. His sister had been an excellent swimmer. She'd taught him how, too, in the creek near their broken-down house. Also, there had been a man who had died, as well. Not her husband.

He couldn't imagine Bunny not being faithful. She'd hated his father—her stepfather—for not being true to their mother.

There was a mystery tied to the scandal. He intended to find out what it was and what had really happened to Bunny, the only person he had ever trusted completely—

"Salad?" the widow asked sweetly, breaking into the dark thoughts that haunted him.

Kate would have been around nineteen, maybe twenty, when his sister and the man with her had died. He hadn't learned about the deaths until he'd become a cop and started a search to find his missing relative. It was a shame Bunny's husband, Sean Windom, had gotten himself killed in a car accident a few years later. Damned bad luck all around.

Jess wondered what Kate knew about the accident, but he wouldn't ask. Not yet. First he wanted to do some undercover investigating before word got around and everyone closed up like clams at a change in the tide. He knew what these small-town people were like. They all banded together when trouble brewed and one of their own was involved. He wasn't sure he suspected skullduggery, but it paid to be cautious.

"Thanks." He managed a tight smile and took the bowl from her. She returned his smile in the same vein. It was as if she were taunting his determination to keep a careful distance.

She should have been inside his head last night. She might not be so smug if she knew the erotic thoughts that had run through his dreams, all of them about her and him.

"Good, huh, Dad?"

Jess relaxed somewhat when Jeremy broke the dangerous trend of thought with his innocent question. "Delicious."

"I cooked the one you're eating. Kate showed me how."

"Well, that was…neighborly."

He caught the smile she held back, and realized she knew he was fighting a totally irrational fury as well as an equally irrational attraction. He cursed silently, letting the bitterness flow, wanting it to drown the need this woman aroused, which he didn't understand.

She was just a woman with gorgeous eyes that made him think of things he hadn't let himself think on in years. He glanced around the yard, the garden, the supper the three of them were sharing in the warmth of the last rays of the sun. To an outsider he was sure they looked like the ideal family. Mom and dad and sonny makes three.

He had once wanted those very things, had dreamed of them, yearned for them, worked at making his life fit that ideal. That was when he'd been a stupid kid, one who thought he could make the world right. He knew better.

Kate and Jeremy were discussing the big ones that got away and arguing over whose had been the largest. He felt the pull of her deep within, in that place where he allowed no one.

No one.

He didn't want any interference in his life, not at this stage of the game. He had all he needed to contend with at present, thank you very much.

Not that fate had ever cared much about *his* wishes.

Chapter Three

Kate heard the truck engine stop. Jeremy, turning the compost heap, looked up, too.

"That must be Dad."

"Uh-huh." She continued pulling weeds out of the row of lettuce while wondering about the detective's trips. After four days of sleeping and lounging around, he had started leaving the ranch each morning at nine and returning around noon. This was the third day in a row for this behavior. She realized it was Thursday, and her guests had been in residence for a week.

And she was certainly no closer to knowing more about them. She refrained from questioning the son. It seemed sneaky.

For the past couple of days, the boy, instead of watching television, had taken to helping her in the garden while his father was gone. In the afternoons the two males fished or rowed around the lake in the john boat she and Jeremy had moved from the barn at the big house down to the lake at Megan's urging. Her cousin had invited Jeremy to come up and ride with her when he felt like it.

Kate thought he was too bashful to go alone, but she hadn't volunteered to accompany him. Jess didn't seem to like seeing his son with her.

She felt the disapproving stare before she turned and met his eyes. Again she was reminded of shadows in a forest, deep green and filled with mysteries she knew nothing of.

"Hi," she called out brightly, putting dazzle in her smile just because his expression was so dour.

He nodded. "Jeremy, I brought you a couple of burgers and some fries. You'd better eat while they're still warm. The bag is in the truck."

Jeremy leaned the shovel against the shed and loped off, casting a thanks to his father over his shoulder. Kate picked up the mound of weeds and tossed them on the compost heap. She realized she was hungry, too.

"Food sounds good. I ate a light breakfast."

"You don't need to skimp on food. You aren't fat," he said, his gaze harsh as he looked her over.

"I didn't mean to indicate I was dieting."

He raised one eyebrow as if questioning just what she did mean.

"What have I done to make you so disapproving?" she asked out of the blue, not realizing, until she spoke the words, how much his attitude irked her.

"You look at me as if I'm a gangster who got off on a technicality."

He shrugged. One hand rested on his right hip. He shifted his weight to that leg and rested the left one while he continued to peruse her old work shirt and the jeans which were out at the knees and full of holes elsewhere.

"Stay away from my son," he said finally and turned his back on her, limping as he headed toward the apartment.

"What?" she said in disbelief. She jumped across three rows of vegetables, caught up with him and grabbed his arm. "Just what the heck did you mean by that?"

He rounded on her. "I mean neither I nor my kid needs you. We don't need nurturing—"

"Maybe you don't, but he does."

"We'll be gone as soon as I..." He stopped and eyed her with distaste. "By the end of the month," he finished. "There's no use in building attachments that won't mean a damned thing."

"You don't want your son to have friends?" she demanded, incredulous at the idea. "Is that what you're saying? You leave him here alone day after day and think he doesn't need someone to talk to?"

A faint flush spread over his neck. "Staying here is his choice. As far as socializing goes, there's no point in it, not with you or anyone here. We won't be here that long." He moved his arm, dislodging her grip.

"Maybe you don't need friends, but he does."

At his derisive snort, a devil took hold of her tongue. "Maybe he and Megan and I will become friends for life. Maybe he'll come visit us in the summer—"

She got no further. He gripped her collar as if she were a suspect being brought to justice and yanked her on her toes until they were within kissing distance. But that wasn't on his mind. He looked dangerous, threatening.

"If any of you does anything to hurt that boy, I'll be all over you like a case of hives, you got that?"

She nodded slowly.

Jess saw fear flicker through her eyes before she tossed her head and flashed him an insolent smile.

"That was real original," she drawled. "Something from an old detective movie you watched on TV this week?"

He had to give her credit for holding her ground, but that crack about his son needing friends got to him. He didn't want Jeremy facing the same disappointments in life he had.

"I don't want any expectations built up in the kid that won't be met. Life is tough enough for the young."

"The way it was for you?"

He cursed at the pity in her eyes even as he felt like crawling into those blue depths and drowning in the promise of fulfillment there. Damn. He didn't know what was wrong with him. She made him think of things…well, he knew better.

Life held no surprises for him, good or bad. It served up the usual fare. He didn't want his son to expect too much, then have his heart broken by lies and promises not kept.

"Just leave me and mine alone," he reiterated and

pushed away from her before he forgot the anger and yielded to the demands of his flesh. Need was in him, mixing with the pain of each step, driving him to fury....

He sighed and wiped the sweat from his face. Life had taken another swipe at him. He wanted Kate Mulholland with every fiber of his being. He wondered if she felt the same.

What the hell was he thinking?

Women. They made a man crazy. That's what he needed to remember. That's all. Nothing else.

Kate showered and dressed in a pair of old sweats and thick socks. The mountain air had grown chilly as soon as the sun had set. She dried her hair and slipped a terry-cloth band around her head to hold it back from her face.

Going downstairs, she padded out on the porch and sat in the swing. The fresh nip in the air toyed with her senses. The quarter moon was up. The western sky wasn't quite dark. Touches of magenta and purple mingled with the blue of twilight.

Sprays of forsythia and flowering quince graced the rock garden she'd made at the corner of the old-fashioned porch. It was her favorite spot at her favorite time of day.

The swing gave off a soft but pleasant squeak with each backward sweep of the chain on its hook. She was comforted by the familiar sound. Tonight she needed comforting. For some reason, the past, with its harsh regrets, crowded her thoughts.

The sky darkened and stars crept out, shyly at first, then more and more until the heavens were filled.

With an effort she staved off the old memories, induced by her tenants, she realized. Jess Fargo and his son reminded her of the possibilities of life, of the family she'd once assumed she would have. Shaking her head slightly, she pushed the cold emptiness of old dreams back into their cubbyhole.

Just as she was thinking it was time to go in to bed, a shadow appeared at the corner of the house, causing every nerve in her body to jump.

Jess limped across the grass and up on the porch. "That swing is driving me nuts," he said by way of explanation. "I brought some grease."

Without another word, he pulled a chair over to the swing, stood on it and oiled the hook. Moving back, he advised her to try it. The swing made no noise when she moved.

"Thanks," she said, injecting sincerity into the word.

"It wasn't for you. It was for me." He moved the chair back to its position, then stood near the steps.

When he didn't leave, she hesitated, then invited him to join her. Expecting him to take the chair, she was startled anew when he settled on the swing with a weary sigh.

"Your leg is bothering you?" she asked, sympathy winning out over other, harder emotions.

"Yeah, and then some," he agreed wryly.

"I know," she said softly, remembering the ache that lasted long after the actual pain disappeared.

"Look," he said, "I didn't mean to sound weird this afternoon. It's just that I'm worried about the boy. He's having a hard time, and he's…vulnerable."

"He needs someone. You, I think. It's good that you've been doing things together."

"You think so?"

She was surprised at the hope in his voice. So the tough cop needed assurances, too. "Absolutely."

After a few minutes he exhaled deeply and relaxed against the wooden slats. She started the swing to moving. They swished back and forth while crickets chirped and the wind whispered of secrets millions of years old.

She heard the lazy caw of a crow in the alders down by the creek. "The wind raven," she murmured.

"What?"

Kate stirred self-consciously. "It's an old story my grandmother told us. She said an Indian woman told it to her grandmother when she was a child. When the raven caws before dawn, when the wind blows down the mountain rather than up the valley, dire happenings are foretold. My grandmother's mother heard the ravens before her husband and son were killed by a falling tree. My grandmother said she heard the crows down by the creek the night her baby died. And the wind was blowing."

As if on cue, the cold night air swept around the eaves with a low moan. Her father had explained the house moaned because it wasn't built right for wind, but as a child, she'd thought the wind and the house knew when tragedy was coming. The hair prickled on the back of her neck.

"Do you believe in myths?"

His voice was as soft, as sorrowful, as that of the wind, its deeper cadence blending with the whisperings of the river alders. The prickle became a tremor that raced through her.

"I believe there are things the mind can comprehend and others that only the heart knows and still others that no one understands." She spoke barely above a whisper herself.

He moved, turning slightly as if to study her, laying his arm along the back of the swing, crossing his sore knee over the other while he watched her. She became uneasy.

"What bothers you about me?" he asked.

The silence grew—a mound of unsaid words between them. "Your unhappiness," she said at last. "Your dislike and disapproval for no reason that I know of."

"I don't dislike you," he said, so low she nearly didn't catch the words.

"Your distrust...of women or everyone?"

His laugh was bitter. "Of life."

"I understand."

"I doubt it." He was back to tough, cynical.

"I was married twelve years ago today. Barely past my twenty-first birthday."

"It wasn't a happy union," he guessed.

"My father didn't want me to, but nothing would have stopped me, not even a gypsy with a genuine crystal ball that showed me what my life would be like if I went through with the ceremony. I probably knew without the crystal ball."

"But you did it, anyway."

"Yes."

"And?"

"We fought the good fight, one might say, but it

didn't work for us. Not all the love or hope or faith in the world could change what was inevitable.''

''You divorced.''

''No. He died.''

''How?''

She heard the sharpened interest of the experienced cop in the question. She couldn't decide how much to tell him or if she wanted him to know. Suicide. She hadn't said the word in four years, and she wasn't sure she could say it now.

''Suicide?'' he said before she could get the word out, again in the deep tone that harmonized with the wind.

A raven cawed. Another answered.

''Yes.'' The emptiness returned and with it the memories of a fate she had been powerless to change, although at twenty-one, she had thought she could. By the time she was twenty-nine, she had known she couldn't.

''Go,'' the raven called from the river bank. ''Go.''

She rose and went inside without another word.

The wind came up during the night, sluicing down the mountain, pouring into the valley, bringing lightning and the promise of rain. At dawn the rain still held off, but the clouds lingered like a lid clamped over the land, holding in the growing tempest.

Kate rose and dressed in fresh jeans, tank top and a long-sleeved flannel shirt. The temperature was in the low fifties. She put on coffee, then ate her usual bowl of cereal.

Standing by the kitchen windows, she watched the wind toss the branches of the alders. The sky was dark, threatening. Along the edge of the mountain nearest her, she stared at the curtain of white without realizing what it was.

"Hail," she said as the first white balls began to hit the glass and skip along the grass. She saw it tear through a leaf of a bush, then knock a flower off another.

The garden! The hail would ruin her carefully tended lettuce and beans and sweet peas. It would rip through the broad leaves of the cucumbers, squash and pumpkins. She slipped into old loafers and ran to the garden shed for the drop cloths that served multiple purposes around a ranch.

The wind beat at her, so hard it felt as if it would tear her clothes from her body. The hailstones, all nearly the size of marbles, hit with ferocious tenacity. She secured a corner of the drop cloth with a rock and tried to cover the row of lettuce. The wind whipped the material from her fingers.

"I'll get it." Jess reached across her and grabbed the flailing cloth and put it into place. "Get one of those big rocks," he told his son.

Between the three of them, they got the most vulnerable vegetables covered. As they ran for the house, the rain started, lashing across the land in long, shimmering curtains.

"Wow, I don't think the weatherman predicted that," Kate said with a laugh once they were safely inside the kitchen. She tossed towels to her helpers, then dried herself off.

She checked her clothing to make sure she was decent. When she glanced up, Jess was watching her. The quickly hidden flare in his eyes told her he remembered their first meeting. His words of the night before leaped into her mind.

Desire flamed in her, echoing her restless night. She missed the heat, the pleasure of sex, the deep satisfaction and closeness afterward. In those early years of marriage, when hope still reigned, she had sought it eagerly. Later she had tried to use it as a bond to help her husband live in the present, but he had retreated more and more into the past, to places where she had never been and couldn't go.

"I have coffee," she said rather abruptly, turning from her guest's steady perusal. "This feels like a pancake-and-sausage morning to me. How about you?"

"Yeah," Jeremy said enthusiastically, pulling the towel over his hair as if he were polishing a shoe. He glanced at his father. "Uh, if we have time."

Only a curmudgeon could have denied the youngster's eager hunger. Kate looked at Jess. The corners of his mouth tightened, but he nodded.

She threw her towel on top of the washing machine in the adjoining room, then started preparing the meal. Jess and Jeremy followed her example but took seats at the table. She served coffee to the older male and cocoa to the younger one.

After they ate, Jeremy asked to be excused. He wanted to check on his e-mail. Kate grinned as he thanked her, then bounded out and across the wet yard, jumping puddles. As soon as he was inside, the rain came pouring down again.

"This might last all day," she informed Jess. "The roads won't be passable at low spots."

"So I shouldn't go to town?"

"I'd give it an hour or so after the rain has stopped for the roads to drain."

"I will. Today seems a good day for staying in and reading, anyway. You have any books?"

"In the study. First door on the right down the hall. Choose anything you like. I'll bring fresh coffee."

When she brought in their mugs, she found Jess standing in front of the bookshelves. He continued to read over the titles. "You have quite a collection of Western lore here."

"My family has collected first editions for generations."

"Some of these might be valuable."

"The ones behind the glass doors are. The others aren't. Except to me."

He moved over to the glass-fronted bookcases. "Mark Twain. Bret Hart. What's this? *Mrs. Beeton's Every Day Cookery and Housekeeping Book*?

"Household hints from 1865," Kate explained. "The author was English."

He glanced through the volume. "It says here that all the household belongs to the husband, and the wife must look after his interests well. Sounds like a sensible female."

Kate frowned in annoyance that he would happen upon that advice out of the whole book. He turned and she saw his smile widen as he took in her expression. She realized he was teasing her. Well, the tough cop had a sense of humor.

"Yes. My father pointed that out to my mother one time," she admitted.

"What did she do?"

"Hit him with the dust mop."

When Jess chuckled, Kate laughed, too. While he selected a couple of police procedural mysteries, she mused on their moment of laughter. It had been a long time since this house had heard the shared laughter of a man and woman.

And longer before it would happen again. She wanted no part of Jess Fargo. She left him in the den and returned to the kitchen, continuing her silent lecture on men and women and the whole absurd misery of it all.

Sitting at the kitchen table, watching the storm worsen, she tried to push the memories back into the past and lock the door. She had always been moody around the time of her wedding anniversary, but this year the hurt seemed nearer the surface.

Because of Jess?

Because somehow he and his son reminded her of all the bright hope she had once held dear to her heart. But she had learned that love wasn't enough. It couldn't change fate.

Touching her abdomen briefly, she experienced the pain of shattered youth and dreams, of accepting the reality, the nightmare, that her life had become…and yet, with the stubbornness of the young, she had dared hope….

Until that terrible, final day.

Needing to be busy, she set about rinsing the plates and putting them in the dishwasher. Her tenant limped into the kitchen, bringing three books tucked under his arm. She said nothing while he refilled his cup and laid the books on the table. He offered to help clean up.

"There's nothing to do." While he sat at the table,

she wiped the skillet and grill with a paper towel and put them away. Restless, she made two cherry pies. With them in the oven, she, too, sat and stared morosely at the rain.

"You're quiet," he mentioned after a long silence. "And introspective. Are you thinking about your marriage?"

"About love."

His face hardened.

"Yeah, I don't think much of the emotion, either. It's a trap for women—"

"You think it isn't for men?" he said in a near snarl.

She shrugged. Their eyes met and held. Behind the smoldering animosity, she saw something else—the hunger, raw and naked, all male, but beyond that—the pure lonely need of one person for another.

She turned her head, refusing to acknowledge the mutual emotion. But it impinged on the mind just the same. It was the same need that gnawed at her.

A hand touched her chin, bringing her back to face him. "It's there. We can deny it, but it's there."

His tone was harsh, and he didn't look at all pleased.

"What?" she asked, lifting her chin defiantly.

"You know."

The silence loomed between them again, silence that screamed with a thousand denials. Then, to her shock, he leaned forward and, light as a dewdrop, he touched his lips to hers.

Hot puffs of desire blew in and out of her. She pressed her lips together to stop the flow. He kissed her again.

She opened her mouth to protest. A mistake. He opened his lips at the same moment. Whether by design or accident, their tongues touched, lightly, hardly more than the flutter of an eyelash. But it hurt. Way down deep somewhere.

They each drew back, startled, eyes wide, nostrils flaring. A gasp, then a shaky sigh escaped her.

"Damn," he said. "This isn't... It isn't enough."

"I know," she admitted weakly, hating herself for it.

His broad hand cupped the back of her head. He held her close, then his mouth was on hers, fierce, demanding, wanting, needing...and she was kissing him back the same way.

She entwined a hand into the thick, dark strands and took the kiss farther, deeper. He groaned and lifted her, turning his chair so he could place her on his lap.

"Your knee—"

"It's okay. Don't fuss," he muttered against her mouth.

The kiss went on. Flesh pressed flesh, consumed the warmth, reveled in the close heat of passion barely held in check. His hands swept under her shirt and tank top. His touch was gentle but urgent on her back as he caressed up and down her spine.

When he moved forward, then pressed her breasts upward and dropped kisses along the curving mounds, she caught her breath as ecstasy flooded her. She rained kisses on his head and raked her fingers through his hair, then slipped them under his collar and down his back.

She wanted all barriers gone. With hands that trembled, she fumbled with his shirt buttons. He impatiently yanked it open, then pulled his T-shirt up and laid her hands flat on his chest and pressed them there.

"Touch me," he whispered, as lost to the moment as she was. "I've wanted it since I first saw you. Maybe forever."

"That makes no sense," she said, trying to regain some control in the maelstrom.

He lifted his head, his expression grim. "It never does."

But he didn't release her hands. Instead he urged her to move them on him. She caressed him eagerly, forgotten pleasure rushing through her at the sensation of rough hair over the smoothness of skin beneath.

He kissed her again, hotly, deeply, his mouth moving over hers, his tongue seeking, demanding, then becoming playful as he enticed her to follow his lead. She didn't know how long or how far they would have gone, except for the ringing of the phone. Every nerve in her body jumped at the sound.

"Easy," he said, resting his forehead against hers.

The phone jangled again.

"It might be important." She wanted him to say it wasn't.

"Yeah." He sighed, gently helped her stand, then did the same. "You want to get it?"

She crossed the room and answered.

"This is Jeremy. Uh, will you tell my dad the library called and they have the stuff from the archives he wanted to see?"

She ran a hand through her hair and tried to smooth

it into place. "Okay. Do you need to speak with him?"

"No. I'm going to catch a movie on television now."

They hung up and she delivered the news. The darkness returned to his eyes, displacing the fires of passion.

"Thanks. I guess I'd better wait until tomorrow to go to town."

"That would be a good idea."

He studied her for a long minute. "Yeah." Then he went out the door.

Kate rubbed her fingers over her lips, which still felt hot and needy. Watch it, she warned herself. Just watch it. She went to the door. "What are you doing here, really?"

He glanced over his shoulder. Raindrops splashed his hair and clothing. "Resting." He hesitated. "I'll be gone at the end of the month." It was a promise.

"Good," she said, and was pretty sure she meant it.

Chapter Four

Jess read the final paragraph of the newspaper article. He slumped into the library chair and absently rubbed his aching leg while he mulled over the report from ten years ago.

There had been no storm, no unusual wind, no sudden change in weather, the day his sister had gone sailing with a local man, Jimmy Herriot, son of Patrick Windom's sworn enemy. Neither had returned from the excursion alive.

He considered the sparse details, then gave it up as his thoughts went in circles. Question after question chased through his mind. No answers, though.

The police write-up on the case should fill in a few of the blanks. He thought of the local detective who'd been so helpful about finding him a place to stay, Shannon Bannock, smiling that secret woman's smile as she sent him to her cousin, the reclusive widow. He'd pictured Kate as a hermit of a woman.

Immediately an image of that first meeting sprang to mind—the sight of her in the wet clothing, the heat that had seared him, the slap of cold water from the writhing hose that hadn't cooled his blood in the least....

He scowled as his body stirred, and longing pierced a sensitive place he'd walled off long ago. Heartsick, his mom had once told him. A longing for things he couldn't have.

Kate was in that category. He'd be gone by the end of the month. That would be the end of this stupid attraction and the restless dreams in which he held her close and shared secrets of the heart. With grim control, he forced the emotion back into the hidden shadows of his soul.

Focusing his attention on the problem at hand, he reread the newspaper reports, then turned his analytic ability to the tragedy. He mulled over the facts and all who had been living at the time.

Kate, Shannon, Megan. Bunny and Sean Windom—his sister and brother-in-law who were also Megan's parents. And then there were the two old men. One was the grandfather of the three cousins and the other the grandfather of the current Herriot heir. Where did they fit into the picture?

According to local gossip he'd gleaned from the old men who gathered to chat every morning at a local café, Patrick Windom had loved a woman named Mary Sloan, but shortly before their wedding day, she had upped and married Sebastian ''Sonny'' Herriot. It was Sonny and Mary's son who had died that day with Bunny. Had they been lovers? Confidantes?

Jess sighed. Another detail that needed checking out. Soon he would have to reveal who he was and make himself known to his only remaining relative besides his son.

Megan Windom. Bunny's child. His niece.

Chill fingers trailed down his spine. The last he'd heard from Bunny was a letter telling him she was about to be married and that she would send for him as soon as she could. Their mother had died that winter from pneumonia. His dad stayed drunk all the time. Jess had been eager to leave.

But then his father had packed up and they'd moved again, one step ahead of the law. He discovered his dad was also a thief. Bunny must have moved, too. His letter, letting her know of *his* move, was returned with no forwarding address. If she wrote again, the letter didn't catch up with him as he and his dad drifted from place to place.

Remembering her admonitions about an education, he'd managed to stay in school and earn good grades. As soon as he graduated, he'd left home and joined the police force of a Houston suburb. When he'd married, when he'd had a son, when he'd made detective, he'd wanted to share the news with Bunny. She would have been proud of him. With the resources of a vice squad commander available to him, he'd decided to find her.

He'd been two years too late.

Sighing, he neatly folded the newspaper, slipped it in its folder and returned it to the librarian. "I can't find the other edition you requested," she told him cheerily. "It's probably misfiled. I'll have one of the volunteers look for it. Shall I call when we locate it?"

"I'll stop in when I'm in town."

"Fine. Have a nice day."

He walked out and stood on the steps of the stone structure. Made from local granite, the library and town hall were the most impressive buildings in town. A grocery, a pharmacy, a beauty and barber shop, a hardware and a farm/ranch store comprised most of the businesses along the main street. A small general store did a thriving business in ranch wear, fishing gear, boots and household items.

According to the sign at the city limits, the place had one thousand residents. He found that hard to believe. There were only a couple of hundred houses scattered along the narrow valley and the bench above it. The Roost Café was the only restaurant, not counting the fast-food places at each end of town. Next door was a bar with a pool table in the back.

Glancing at his watch, he saw it was past noon. He crossed the street and went inside the noisy diner. Business was brisk as usual. One of the old-timers waved him over. He joined the man and two of his friends in a booth.

"How's your leg doing?" Mr. Burleson asked.

"Better."

"You getting some sun on it like I told you?"

"Yes, an hour a day, just like you said."

Mr. Burleson gave nearly toothless smile of approval. "Nothing like the sun to bake the pain out of your bones and keep you from getting arthritis. Did I tell you about the time I was trampled?"

Without waiting for an answer, he launched into an

account of his cow-punching days and getting caught in a stampede. Jess listened patiently. He'd heard the story, but he didn't mind indulging the old man. Burleson and his cronies were the ones who'd told him about the man with Bunny and the enmity between the Herriots and the Windoms.

After lunch, he drove to the apartment. Jeremy was watching an old movie on television.

"You had lunch?" Jess asked.

"Yeah. Me an' Kate ate up at the big house."

"At the big house," Jess repeated, not liking the idea of Jeremy going to the Windom mansion, for some reason.

Surliness darted over his son's face. "Kate took me up to ride," the boy said. "Megan said I could help with the horses. She's going to pay me."

There was pride and defiance in the boy's expression. Jess considered the situation. The truth was he didn't want Jeremy involved with the Windom family. Not while he was investigating them for a possible murder rap.

Murder.

He admitted the word into his consciousness for the first time, although it had been floating around the back of his mind since he'd found out about the drowning accident. There were a lot of blanks in this puzzle. He needed to see those police reports. Unless they'd been purged.

There was that possibility. He knew how politics affected justice. People covered up for friends and influential citizens all the time. He'd seen it in the police department, the D.A.'s office, the courts, in every public sphere.

"You haven't had riding lessons," he reminded the boy.

"Kate said I had a natural seat," Jeremy said, enthusiasm replacing the resentment in his eyes. "And her cousin is going give me some pointers and teach me to jump."

Jess couldn't bring himself to put a crimp in the boy's happiness. The kid had had little enough during the past few months. He nodded and tried to look pleased.

He limped out on the deck over the garage, settled on a recliner that was half in, half out of the shade and bared his aching knee to the sun. The heat was soothing. He fell asleep.

Kate was puzzled. Moreover, she was suspicious, and she hated being that way. She hated not trusting people. She hated having to question their motives and acts. It was the way she'd spent the last years of her marriage.

But there was probably nothing suspicious about her tenant and his reading of back copies of the local newspaper. Yeah, and if she believed that, maybe she ought to buy the Brooklyn Bridge with her life savings.

She whipped into the garage, then ran up the steps to the apartment. Inside she could see Jeremy lying on the sofa. She thought he was asleep. She'd already spied his father on the deck, so she quietly crossed to the sliding glass door and closed it behind her.

Jess opened his eyes as she stepped outside. The glance he gave her wasn't welcoming.

While he pulled the recliner back to an upright position, she stalked over to the patio table and turned a chair around to face him. "Why are you reading old newspaper stories about my family?" she asked, making her tone curious rather than accusatory and demanding.

He took a fair time about answering. "I was interested." As if sensing this wasn't going to satisfy her, he added, "Being here, meeting you and your cousins, I was curious about the history of the Windraven ranch."

"Why?"

"Your story about the ravens. Then Tom Burleson mentioned something about it."

She rolled her eyes at the name. "Those old gossips."

Jess smiled without humor. "They come in handy, those old men and their memories. They knew I'd rented the apartment. It reminded them of the tragedies your family has gone through."

"What did Tom and his friends tell you?"

"They said the ravens cawed the night before the drowning, that everyone in the valley heard and worried about their loved ones because it foretold tragedy within twenty-four hours."

"So you went to the library and read up on Aunt Bunny's drowning and Uncle Sean's auto accident?" Kate asked.

The librarian had told Kate those were the back issues of the weekly newspaper that he'd requested. He hadn't checked on Kris's suicide, as she'd expected when Mrs. Ellison had mentioned her renter coming in and making inquiries. Instead he'd been interested in Sean's and Bunny's tragedies. Why?

"The drowning, yes. The librarian couldn't find the paper detailing the auto accident." He watched her, his face expressionless, for a long ten seconds, then, "Why does that bother you?" he asked.

"I don't know," she said truthfully. "It's meddling, for one thing. And it seems old. You have no right—"

"More than you think," he broke in.

Their eyes locked in a power struggle she didn't understand. Suspicion increased. "Who are you?" she demanded.

He sighed and closed his eyes briefly. Meeting her gaze levelly, he muttered, "It will all be out soon, anyway."

"What will?"

"Who I am," he answered cryptically.

She waited, fear crawling up her neck for no reason she could define, just that gut feeling she'd always gotten just before her husband went berserk again.

"Bunny Windom was my sister."

"Bunny...Aunt Bunny?" It made no sense. "Her name wasn't Fargo."

"It was Vickers. We had different fathers." His laugh was cynical. "She got the good one."

Kate shook her head as she processed this latest, totally unexpected information. "But that would mean...that means you're Megan's uncle."

"Yes."

Kate slumped into the chair, her stuffing knocked out by the news. "You haven't told her. For all these years she thought she had no one left from her mother's family. Why didn't you contact her?"

Obviously reluctant to disclose information, he told

her of his past and of losing track of his sister while he and his father drifted from one town to another, mostly in Texas and Oklahoma. "When I found out she died in a sailing accident, there seemed no point in pursuing it further. I wasn't sure she'd ever told her new family about us. I didn't blame her for that," he added cynically.

"We knew she was from Texas. And that her life had been difficult. She met Uncle Sean while waiting tables. He was a senior at the university at the time. She was taking classes, too. They married as soon as he graduated. I loved her as soon as they arrived here when I was six. She was beautiful…and kind."

Kate saw pain flash through his eyes. From his terse explanation, she concluded his father had been a drifter and that he had loved his sister. Losing track of her had probably seemed like abandonment to him.

"Did you see a lot of her?" he asked. He pulled his pants leg down over his knee and scooted his chair backward into the shade of the walnut trees.

"Not a lot," she told him. "I was six when Uncle Sean married. I was nineteen when Aunt Bunny died. My own mother was dying of cancer. Other than her and my father, I didn't pay a lot of attention to the other adults in the family."

He nodded and rubbed his leg. "It's all probably immaterial at this date. But I was curious…"

"Why do you want to know about Uncle Sean's accident?"

"The man was my brother-in-law. It seemed natural. I wondered what he was like."

Kate stared into the distance, her mind searching back on the past. "I think he must have loved Aunt

Bunny very much. After her death, he sort of went to seed, you might say. He started drinking. He and Grandfather quarreled about it. He was drunk when he died. Luckily he didn't hurt anyone else.''

"Maybe that was his intention—to kill only himself.''

Tears filled her eyes. "Megan was so young when her mother died and only sixteen when Uncle Sean wrapped himself around a bridge abutment. Grandfather had a stroke the day after the funeral. He hasn't walked since.''

"I'm sorry.''

She studied Jess. His gaze was sincere, even sympathetic. "You loved your sister very much,'' she said softly.

"She was all the good things in life,'' he answered simply.

The tragedies of her own life sifted through her. "Necessary losses,'' Judith Viorst had called them in her book. Kate had read it and clung to the knowledge that all humans suffered death and pain in their lives. That didn't lessen the hurt but it helped make living bearable. "We all have losses. It's the price for living.''

"But for some, death comes prematurely,'' he said in a harsh tone, his face grim.

"Like Bunny? Because she drowned?''

"She was an excellent swimmer.''

Kate caught the undertone of suspicion. "You think it wasn't an accident?'' she asked, shocked by the implication.

He turned his head and stared at the roof of the big house, visible above the trees. "I don't know.'' He sighed moodily. "It probably was. Maybe I've been a cop too long."

"The boat sprang a leak. The authorities decided Aunt Bunny got hit by the boom. She had a blow on her head. Jimmy Herriot had several broken ribs. One pierced his heart. They thought he'd cut too sharply into the wind when he'd realized there was a problem and had overturned the boat, causing the injuries as they went down. They capsized on the rocks."

"Yeah, that's what the newspaper said."

"But you still have questions."

He shook his head negatively, but his eyes were pensive.

Pity tugged at her heart. She rose before she did something stupid like reach over and stroke his arm or brush the lock of thick, dark hair off his forehead. "When are you going to tell Megan who you are?"

"Soon. Today," he added, when she frowned at him.

"In person or by phone?"

"Phone."

Kate considered. "No. I'll call and invite her to dinner. You and Jeremy can come, too. Then he and I will do the dishes while you explain everything to her."

He looked as if he would argue, but after a second he nodded agreement. "What time?"

"Seven." She hurried toward the sliding door. "I'll call her now."

However, the phone was ringing when Kate entered the house. She caught it before the answering machine clicked on. "Hello?"

She was half expecting it to be Jess with some

argument about why they couldn't tell Megan his news just yet.

It was Shannon. "Oh, good, you're home," she said in relief. "Katie, love, I have a big favor to ask—"

"No," Kate said, knowing from Shannon's manner that it was a favor she wouldn't like.

"I wouldn't ask if it wasn't an emergency. You know I wouldn't. But it's really important."

"How many?" Kate asked.

Shannon was silent for a moment. "Just one."

"How old?"

"Three."

"No."

"Her mother died recently. Her father broke out of jail. Inmates say he's coming for the child, that he's going to kill her, then himself."

Kate gripped the phone with both hands. "I don't want to know. Find someone else, Shannon. I can't, not now."

Shannon let go a long breath in disappointment. "Okay, Kate. Sorry I called. I didn't mean to upset you."

"I'm not..." Kate didn't finish the lie. "Who will you get to keep her? Mrs. Harris?"

"She's got the Chaney twins."

"Oh."

The mother of the eight-year-old twin boys left them at the police station every couple of years and disappeared for a month. Then she would return and be fine for months or years before she just had to go "find herself" again.

Kate had kept them the first couple of times when

they were babies. That was before her husband had gotten so bad and she'd been afraid to have children around him. The little ones seemed to drive whatever demons had haunted Kris into fury. She'd been worried when she'd realized she was pregnant, but he had seemed okay at the time. He'd been sane for months.

"I'll call around," Shannon said. "Maybe I can find someone. The problem is that people are afraid when I tell them about the father. I really need a safe house…. But it's not your problem. I'll talk to you later. Bye for now."

Kate said goodbye and hung up. Her breath sounded sharp and too fast in the empty room. She inhaled deeply, let it out, then inhaled again. She jammed her gardening hat on her head and went outside. She needed air…space…

Looking up, she encountered shadowed green eyes watching her as she grabbed the hoe. She nodded curtly and headed for the corn patch. An hour of weeding would take care of the spurt of nervous energy Shannon's call had induced.

Jess stood at the open door, not sure whether he was relieved or disappointed. Kate had reported Megan was busy that evening and couldn't come to dinner. She had arranged for all of them to have lunch the next day.

He watched her weeding her garden with a vengeance. He was surprised at how upset she was at learning who he was and his connection to the family. Maybe she thought he and Bunny weren't good enough—

No. Kate wasn't like that. She was the sun, spreading her warmth equally on all around her. She'd become a friend to his son, which the boy needed. She was someone Jeremy could trust.

That hard yearning he'd discovered of late grew to fill his chest, making it difficult to breathe. He suddenly wished he'd met Kate Chandler Mulholland years ago, before either of them had married, before they'd been disillusioned, before his life had ended in a shot to the knee....

He scowled, surprised and angry with the thought. No good came of dreaming about things that could never be.

"Hey, Dad."

Jess faced his son. His heart squeezed down to the size of a walnut as he studied the gangly youth. Most of all, he wished he could erase the wariness from the boy's eyes, the tentative way his son always approached him, as if checking to see if it was safe to come close.

An ache ran all through him. This was his son, his promise to the future. The feelings he'd had the first time he'd held the baby in his arms, the dreams of them as a family, his vow to be the best father, all had come to nothing.

"Yeah, son?" he said past the pain in his throat.

"I thought I might run up to the stables and see if, um, they needed some help."

Jess had noticed that Jeremy called the cousins by their first names when talking to them, but he usually used the generic "they" when talking to him about the women, either individually or collectively. "Be back before supper," he said, giving his permission.

"Sure." The boy grabbed a cap, put it on backward and was down the stairs an instant later.

Jess returned to his contemplation of Kate working in her garden. When she stopped and wiped sweat from her forehead on her sleeve, he went to the refrigerator, poured two glasses of iced tea and limped down the steps.

"Hey," he called, setting the glasses on the picnic table.

Kate looked his way. With a slight frown she walked to the shed, cleaned the hoe and put it away before joining him.

"Thanks," she said and lifted the glass.

"Jeremy went up to the stables. Is that okay, or did he misunderstand your cousin's invitation?"

"Megan asked him to help. She volunteered to pay him. I'd say the arrangements are between them."

Her tone carried no inflection that he could detect. It was as if she had detached herself from the present and retreated to a place he couldn't reach. He gave a cynical snort. There was no reason for him to reach her. He'd be gone before anything happened between them.

He nodded and kept silent. Around them, bees hummed busily as they moved around the garden, paused at blue spikes of larkspur or snuggled into a sweet pea. Ants dashed along a more or less straight line in their zig-zaggy, stop-and-start manner, conferring with other ants as they returned to the nest and nurtured their young.

"I think..." she said, then stopped.

He waited, sure he wasn't going to like whatever she was going to say.

"I think it would be better if you found another place to stay," she concluded, her gaze riveted on the alders and cottonwoods along the creek that flowed into the lake.

He digested this news, studied it from several angles and decided not to make it easy for her, although on some level he thought the same. "Why?"

She looked at him, her gaze candid, as usual, her eyes so beautiful they almost made a man forget what he was doing.

"Because we're dangerous to each other's peace of mind. Because you're going to be here another three weeks, and I'm not sure I can hold out that long."

He let his breath out in a whoosh. "You don't pull punches, do you?" he murmured.

"Megan will invite you to stay at the big house when she knows who you are. That will work out for all concerned. You and she will have a lot of catching up to do, so it would be better if you were there. Jeremy would love that. It's closer to the horses."

Her smile was so unexpected it dove right to the center of his being, awakening the hunger and making him aware of her sweet scent wafting across the table on the afternoon breeze. He watched the wind shift the silky tendrils at her temples and had an urge to kiss her there where the blue veins ran under her lightly tanned skin. He had always thought a woman looked fragile and vulnerable at her temples.

"So, you'll leave?" she asked when he didn't speak.

"No," he said, feeling stubborn. "We're settled in here. I don't want to move Jeremy again so soon. Besides, I'm paid up to the end of the month."

"I'll refund your money."

He shook his head. "Sorry, but I like the privacy. Jeremy and I can eat when we like, sleep when we like. The apartment fits our needs."

She clamped her lips together. He noticed how her mouth naturally turned up at the corners, making even her frowns seem friendly and kind.

Pity, he reminded himself. Whether she admitted it or not, Kate was a sucker for a sob story.

"I was thinking of going to Florida and visiting my father and stepmother."

"Fine. Jeremy and I will keep an eye on the place."

She glared at him in frustration.

"I'm not going to run, Kate," he said softly. "You're afraid of what's between us. So am I. But we're adults. We can handle it."

She dropped her head forward and stared at the line of ants. "What if, some night, we're weak at the same time?"

"We deal with it."

"I don't want to. I don't want to deal with passion or emotion or any of that. Not again."

He didn't like being lumped in the same boat with her crazy husband. Getting up, he limped to her side of the table. Following an impulse stronger than common sense, he sat beside her, then laid his hand along her jaw and turned her face to his. "Is this what you mean?"

Claiming her surprised mouth, he held the kiss to gentleness when everything in him clamored for urgency and hot, wild sharing.

"See?" he said, drawing back slightly, his breath coming more rapidly. "No problem."

Her laugh was shaky, disbelieving.

"If we wanted, we could go even farther. Like this."

This time he ran his tongue along the firm seam of her lips, liking the contrast between the softness of her mouth and firmness as she resisted.

He sucked her bottom lip between his teeth and bit down, not hard, but enough to make her gasp in surprise. Then he invaded, a controlled, gentle invasion composed of little flickers, like a hummingbird sipping from a rose. Her mouth was sweet. He'd missed the taste of her...

Against his chest he felt the sudden rapid beat of her heart. His own heart raced. The old sensation of meeting danger and facing it surged through him. He knew he was playing with fire, but it was okay. He was in control.

Kate moaned as heat slithered through her, insinuating itself in every part of her body. She relaxed and let the flame spread, knowing it would go no farther than a simple kiss.

The muscles in his arms hardened as he tightened the embrace. A flicker of concern ran through her, then disappeared. No, it was okay. They were in control.

When he lifted his head, she opened her eyes and watched him, her eyelids heavy.

"You see," he said huskily. "It's just a kiss, nice but not mind-blowing."

"We won't do mind-blowing," she murmured. "It's too dangerous, right?"

"Right."

Jess dipped his head and touched her mouth once more. Lifting her legs, he laid them across his thighs. A lighthearted recklessness swept over him. His mind went a bit hazy as she returned the kiss, turning so that her breasts poked into his chest, searing him with heat and need. It was criminal for a woman to feel this good....

A prickle of unease caressed the back of his neck. What was he trying to prove?

"This is very close to mind-blowing," Kate warned at one point. She was panting lightly, the way she'd done while working in her garden. A sheen of perspiration broke out all over her as flames ran madly through her body.

She furrowed her fingers in his hair and let the strands flow through her fingers like fine silk. His scent filled her—shampoo, aftershave lotion, the fresh-laundered aroma of his T-shirt and a spicy talc. She inhaled deeply.

He groaned and held her closer. His hands caressed her back and along her sides. She twisted at the same time he moved. His wide palm cupped her breast.

"Still with me?" he whispered.

"Yes," she said just as softly.

"See? We can handle this."

"It's only physical."

"Right. Mind over matter."

Jess stared into her eyes and felt the world slip off its axis. Just a bit. A tiny tilt that spoke of passion in check, held tightly on the leash of his self-control. He wondered if the tilt meant he was losing it.

No. He was still thinking clearly...pretty clearly.

"We would have to go much farther," he told her, planting kisses along her temple, "before losing control."

She kissed his chin, down his throat. Flames erupted when he felt the hot lick of her tongue on his skin. When she slid her hands under his shirt and caressed his back, a shower of sparks flared behind his closed eyelids. He thought of cool things—snow, icy waterfalls, hailstones—and tried to hold on.

Kate didn't know when the kiss changed, when it became a challenge to breach the walls of his control. She just knew at some point the situation reversed for her. She wanted more.

"How far?" she asked. "Show me."

He made a sound in the back of his throat, one of surprise when she took the kiss deeper, delving into his mouth with a sudden urgency as need consumed her. Here, in his arms, she felt bold and confident.

"We could do this," he said.

He grabbed the T-shirt at the back of his neck and pulled it over his head. He unfastened the buttons of her work shirt. Watching her, his eyes dark with passion, he slowly merged their bodies, flesh to hot flesh.

He brushed from side to side, causing her breasts to tighten painfully. She wrapped her arms around his shoulders and closed her eyes.

"Yes," she said. "Yes."

Her pulse sounded loudly in her ears. She ran her hands over his back and down his sides. Encountering his jeans, she slid her fingers inside the waistband—

"No," he said hoarsely, catching her hands in his. "This is as crazy as we get."

"The limit," she said, understanding what he meant.

A shudder passed from him to her. "Yeah, the limit."

He moved her away and stood up. The reaction of his body was plain. He cursed under his breath. "Maybe this isn't going to be as easy to handle as I thought," he admitted, a trace of weary humor in the statement.

Triumph flared briefly before she raised her head and met his troubled gaze. "Maybe you'd better reconsider moving."

He shook his head as he limped toward the apartment.

"Stubborn," she said to his back.

"I don't run from anyone," he said in a harsh voice. He walked on.

She laid a hand against her pounding heart. "Maybe running makes good sense in this case," she said softly, a harsh warning to her own clamoring needs. Maybe she really should go to Florida and visit her dad and stepmom for the rest of the month. But she knew she wouldn't.

Chapter Five

Kate woke with a headache the next morning. Midnight had come and gone before she had felt sleepy enough to go to bed.

It was *his* fault. His we-can-handle-this attitude had rankled. Maybe he could. She couldn't. The kiss had stirred too many latent desires within her, plus the old dreams she didn't want disturbed. Her dreams tended to became nightmares.

She recalled another time—standing in the backyard, talking softly to the man she slept with but no longer knew, desperately searching for words that would reach through his insatiable anger at the world, walking slowly toward him, talking…talking….

And then the sound of the shotgun, echoing all around her. The pellets entered her body like a thousand shooting stars.

Time had slowed. Part of her had stood apart from the scene, observing as she slipped to her knees, her face contorted in surprised disbelief. In slow motion she watched herself clasp her hands over her abdomen, already knowing it was too late. Their child, their hope for the future, was no more. The anguish of that moment lived with her still.

Even after she slumped to the ground, she watched as the man, stunned at what he had done, turned the gun on himself and pulled the trigger on the other barrel.

Don't, she warned herself as pain, fresh as the moment it happened, washed over her. The past was gone. There was nothing she could have done to stop the tragedy. Nothing. And that was the worst of all—feeling helpless to deal with Kris, with fate, with the rush of hot, stinging lead that had destroyed the one thing she had cherished....

Closing her eyes, she pressed the heels of her hands against them and willed the memories to stop. The frigid ache of emptiness was easier to bear than the return of longing.

Remembering Jess's arrival, she wondered why she hadn't been as frightened when a total stranger had come around the corner of the house, gun at the ready.

Because his eyes hadn't been crazed with fury. Because he had looked sane and capable and in control. After an initial flash of fear, she had known she could trust him.

But he was dangerous to her in another way. He made her yearn for things she'd lost—her faith in life, her belief in love between a man and a woman, the unfailing certainty that the family was the center of civilization.

Her hands trembling slightly, she prepared one piece of toast and a poached egg, then sat at the table and ate without noticing the food. When she finished breakfast, she turned on the irrigation system that Kris had installed for her and watered the vegetables. He, too, had liked working in the garden or the yard. It had sometimes brought peace to his tormented soul.

Putting the past, including last night's kiss, firmly behind her, she returned to the house. After slipping a pan of brownies and an apple pie in the oven, she cleaned house in preparation for her luncheon guests. By eleven she had everything ready.

She took a quick shower and changed to blue slacks and a white cotton-knit top. Hearing a car in the driveway, she left her hair to fall into its natural waves and hurried downstairs.

A black-and-white sheriff's SUV stopped beside the lawn. Shannon waved at the kitchen window. Pressing a hand against her racing heart, she went outside. Shannon, now at the other door of the vehicle, unbuckled her passenger and lifted a child into her arms.

"This is Amanda," she said, coming across the grass.

Kate didn't speak. She stared at the three-year-old who stared solemnly back at her. The child had big brown eyes the color of dark chocolate. Her brown-black hair lay in ringlets around her face. She had pink cheeks and tawny skin and was a chubby, healthy-looking youngster.

"Amanda, this is Kate. Can you say hello?"

The child buried her face in Shannon's neck.

"She's a tad shy," Shannon said, entering the house.

Kate followed in a daze, her mind in a whirl of protests and anger with Shannon for showing up like this, for knowing how vulnerable she was to a child.

"In fact," Shannon continued, settling in a chair with Amanda in her lap, "she hasn't said but a few words since a neighbor found her sitting beside her mother's body."

"Oh, Shannon," Kate said, holding up a hand as if to ward off the images conjured by the words.

Shannon had the grace to look guilty. "I know. This is terribly unfair of me, but I'm desperate. I can't find anyone willing to take her. She can't stay in the hospital forever."

"Hospital? Is she injured?"

"No. She's right as rain, healthwise, but she was too young for the detention center."

"My God," Kate said in horror.

"I know. We've kept her in the hospital for observation for a week. Now we need a safe place for her."

"And this was the only one you could think of."

"Yes."

Kate watched as Amanda looked around the kitchen, the child's gaze darting here and there as if searching for unknown dangers. So young and already afraid of life. Kate frowned, thinking of the pain parents inflicted on their children, perhaps without meaning to. And then there were the monsters like the escaped convict who intended to harm his child.

A hollow ache permeated her body. She shook her head, denying the need to cuddle the youngster, who should have been busily exploring her new environment with the natural curiosity of the young.

"How long?" she finally asked.

"Only until we catch the father," Shannon assured her in obvious relief. "And find a place for her."

"If Mrs. Harris becomes available, promise me you'll come and get her." She nodded at the girl.

"I will. I promise. Oh, Katie, thank you so much! I hated to ask you, but I was that desperate."

Kate gave a fatalistic shrug. "You may as well stay for lunch. Megan's coming down. My renters are joining us. I think Jess will have some news you'll be interested in."

"Jess?"

"Jess Fargo. The detective you sent."

Shannon eyed her like a cop with a suspect. "Sounds as if you two are friends."

"His son and I are friends. The father is a different cup of tea. He's grouchy, irritable and has a chip on his shoulder, particularly regarding women."

Shannon set Amanda on her feet. "But other than that, what else do you like about him?"

Their eyes met, then Shannon laughed. Kate reluctantly joined in. "He is interesting...as a clinical study."

"Right," Shannon agreed. "Handsome, too."

"If you like the moody, silent type."

"And you don't?"

"No," Kate said bluntly. She set the table, studied Amanda, then cut up a fruit salad and mixed a box of vanilla pudding. She put some cereal in a bowl and held it out to the child. "Do you like cereal?" she asked softly, dropping down to her knees. Her smile felt crimped at the corners.

Amanda watched her with those heart-melting eyes, then picked out one piece and put it in her mouth, so wary and careful it broke Kate's heart.

"Good," Kate said. "Here, hold this." She thrust the bowl into Shannon's hand and proceeded with the lunch preparations.

At exactly twelve, Megan arrived. She was riding one horse and had another on a lead. Kate figured she planned for Jeremy to join her in a ride that afternoon.

Jeremy bounded down the stairs from the apartment. "Wow," he called to Megan. "He's a beaut."

"Want to put him through his paces this afternoon?"

"Sure."

Jess followed his son at a much slower pace. His limp was more pronounced, Kate thought. Maybe he'd had a restless night, too. Which served him right.

"Hi, Shannon. Who's this?" Megan asked, leading the way inside and gesturing toward Amanda. Without waiting for an answer, she dropped to her haunches and beamed a big smile on the child. "Hi, there, brown eyes. I'm Megan. What's your name?"

Amanda froze, one hand clutched on Shannon's pants leg.

Megan glanced at Shannon in question.

"Amanda doesn't talk much. Her mother died recently. She's very sad about that." Shannon tilted her head toward Kate. "But I think that will change soon. Once she's in a stable home and feels a little more certain about things."

Megan's gaze darted between the cousins. "Kate is going to take her?"

"For a while," Kate said. "Until Shannon can find someone more...suitable."

"Good," Megan said, nodding thoughtfully. She stood. "I think that's a very good idea, having someone to keep you company. You're alone too much."

Kate managed a smile. "I'm outnumbered here. Shannon, did you meet Jeremy?"

She introduced the two, then turned to Jess, who had arrived on her door step. "Come in," she invited. "You remember my cousin, the cop, don't you?"

"Quite well." He smiled at Shannon. "You were right. This is the perfect place to rest and recuperate."

Shannon beamed.

But wait until she hears the rest of your news, Kate thought to herself. Shannon and Megan were in for a shock.

Exhaling sharply as unexpected pain hit her, Kate placed a platter of grilled chicken salad, made with fresh greens from the garden, on the table along with a loaf of hot French bread and a pesto pasta dish Megan particularly liked.

"What can Amanda sit on?" Shannon asked, glancing around. "She's not tall enough to reach the table."

"The telephone book," Jeremy suggested.

Megan walked over to a drawer and removed the county telephone directory, which was not quite a half-inch thick. "Will this do?" she asked innocently.

Jeremy and the cousins laughed.

Kate smiled. "Here," she said, placing a thick catalog on the chair. "This should do it."

* * *

During the meal, Jess mulled over a reaction that had startled him. His heart had seized up when Jeremy laughed with Megan and Shannon over the telephone book. Besides startling him, it had stirred a pit of yearning he'd carefully avoided for years. He wished he could go back and get to know his child all over again. His ex had made his visitation rights as difficult as she could, and, not wanting any more trouble, he had acceded to her wishes.

But maybe that was an excuse. These women seemed to have no trouble connecting to the youngster.

Jess observed the three cousins with a jaundiced eye while they ate. Shannon and Megan watched Kate while keeping up a light banter between themselves. There was concern in their eyes for their cousin, but they included Jeremy in their good-natured teasing. His son joined in with an ease that Jess found surprising. The boy's social skills were better than his own.

Kate was nearly silent and ate very little. Each time her eyes flicked to the little girl seated between her and Shannon, he saw pain and regret and hopelessness—emotions he had come to know intimately since his injury.

Was she thinking of her husband who had committed suicide four years ago? Had she witnessed the trauma, unable to prevent it? And why did the presence of a child recall those memories?

There was a mystery surrounding Kate. He wanted to know what it was. But that wasn't his objective in being there. The questions he had regarding Bunny's death came first.

"You ready to take on the Arabian?" Megan asked as soon as the meal was finished.

"Sure," Jeremy responded eagerly.

"You two are going to have fun while I'm stuck in the office the rest of the afternoon," Shannon complained, her sunny smile belying the words.

"Jeremy has to take care of Amanda while I do the dishes," Kate put in firmly.

Jess realized she was trying to make things easy for him. He both appreciated it and was resentful. Which didn't make a hell of a lot of sense. "I need to talk to Megan," he said.

It was almost comical the way all action stopped, a freeze frame of startled attention. Jeremy and the other two women stared at him. The little girl watched them all.

"Me?" Megan said, obviously confused.

"Yes. Please."

Shannon frowned and looked as if she would protest, but Kate shook her head. The cousin subsided. "Well, I've got to get back to work. Call me," she said, looking at Kate, then Megan. The other two nodded.

After Shannon departed, he rose and gestured toward the outside. Puzzled, Megan followed him to the picnic table under the tree, far enough away from the kitchen windows that they wouldn't be heard. They settled across from each other.

She looked at him expectantly.

His heart contracted again. "You have your

mother's eyes,'' he said softly, sorrow rising in him, a tide of regret for things that could never be.

"My...my mother? Did you know her?''

He nodded. "A long time ago. I have a story to tell you. Will you listen?''

"Of course.''

Her face had gone pale. All the earlier gaiety fled. In its place he saw the worry he'd witnessed in his sister when she'd held his hands and told him she was leaving.

I love you better than anyone in the whole world.

"I loved her more than anything,'' he said, unable to control the harsh emotion in his voice. "Even more than the mother that we shared.''

Megan's mouth dropped open in a silent gasp.

"Yeah, she was my sister. We had different fathers, though. Hers was the good one. She told me stories of the things they did as a family. I used to pretend he was my father, too. My dad was lazy, moody and inclined to drink. He didn't hold a job for very long. Mom had to work to keep us in food. Bunny was ten years older and took care of me most of the time.''

He told of Bunny's leaving, his mother's death, his father's rapid descent into alcoholism and thieving. When he finished his tale, tears stood in Megan's eyes. "Mother was good and generous and caring.''

The statement sounded like a question. "Yes,'' he said.

She stared at him, then at the mountains beyond the lake. He was silent, letting her absorb the news at her own pace.

In the garden, bees droned sleepily in the warm afternoon sun. Through the open door, he could see

Jeremy helping Kate with the dishes while the little girl sat on the floor and watched them.

A sort of peace descended on his soul, an unexpected blessing, as if he'd dislodged a burden he hadn't been aware he was carrying. Here, in this isolated place, he felt a sense of family. He wished it could last and knew it couldn't. At the end of the month he would be gone. He'd better stick to that plan. He was a man with no future—

"So you came to find her?" his niece asked.

"No. I knew about the accident." He rubbed his aching knee. "When I was put out of commission, I decided to use the time productively. I wanted to find out exactly what happened, if possible. That last day...would you tell me what you remember?"

She closed her eyes and shook her head. "Nothing."

"Nothing? The newspaper report said you were home with your father and grandfather at the time."

"I was."

"What did Bunny...your mother...say when she left? Did she tell you goodbye, say anything that would indicate she wasn't planning to return?"

"I don't remember."

He stifled impatience. "Start with that morning. What did you have for breakfast? Was Bunny with you?"

"You don't understand," Megan whispered. "I don't remember anything...nothing before the funeral. It's as if I awoke from a long sleep...."

Understanding dawned. "You were eleven years old. Are you saying you don't remember anything about that day? Or don't you recall the first eleven years?''

"The eleven years.''

A chill ran down his spine.

"It's haunted me ever since. My father used to tell me not to worry about it, that someday I would wake up and remember everything. He said losing one's mother was a traumatic thing for a child and he should have been more attentive to me during that time, but he was lost in his own grief.''

Jess felt as if he'd hit a brick wall. Megan had been his main hope for some bit of enlightening information about that odd tragedy. Now there was nothing. He felt the emptiness inside and realized he'd expected a sense of reconnection with his sister. The sudden hot burning behind his eyes startled him. He wasn't a kid. He couldn't burst out crying because some vague childish hope had been blasted to hell. He buried the emotion and concentrated on the facts.

Megan shook her head helplessly. "I want to remember. I want to! Then maybe the nightmares would go away....''

"What nightmares? Describe them to me.''

She stared at him—his blood kin whose eyes were so like her mother's. Her hands were clasped so tightly they had mottled to red and white patches. He hesitated, then laid his hand over hers.

"It's okay. You don't have to talk about it,'' he murmured, angry with fate for bringing him this far only to slap him in the face with this latest development.

She took his hand in both of hers and pressed it to her cheek. "I knew there was something familiar about you and Jeremy. You have her eyes, too, the dark green with the charcoal outline. Like mine. Like my mother's.''

"You remember her eyes?'' he asked carefully.

"Yes. They were so sad…oh!'' She released his hand and pressed her fingers over her mouth. "I think I do. But maybe I think that because I've looked at her picture so much. My father had a portrait painted of her before I was born.''

Jess nodded grimly. "Meeting me may trigger the memories. Don't push it. Sometimes these things come all at once, sometimes a bit at a time.''

She stared at him thoughtfully. "It's so strange, thinking I was alone all these years.''

"You have your cousins.''

"And my grandfather. He's in a wheelchair—''

"I know. Can he communicate at all?''

"Not much. The stroke was a bad one.''

"Your father's death hit him hard,'' Jess suggested.

"Yes. He suffered the stroke a day after the funeral. Did you know that?''

"I read the story in the local paper. The reporter was more interested in reporting superstitions than facts.''

"The ravens,'' she said. Her gaze dropped to the table. "I heard them, too. I couldn't sleep….'' She swallowed hard as the pain hit her eyes again.

Jess discounted this memory. She'd been sixteen at the time her father had wrapped himself around the bridge abutment, an age vulnerable to suggestion and myths. "You were young. It was a hard time for you, as well.''

"I had Kate,'' Megan said in a quiet tone. "She

was always there for me. And for Shannon when her parents divorced and her mother died soon afterward.''

She let out a weary breath and shook her head slightly as if dispersing the dark cloud of death that hung over the family. Jess touched her hand lightly, then withdrew.

''I wish I had been here,'' he said.

She rose and came around the table. He stood, too. To his surprise, she hugged him hard. ''I wish you had, too. I'm glad you came now.'' She drew away, sniffed back tears and smiled. ''I think I'm going to enjoy my new relatives, especially my new cousin. I always wanted a brother.''

''Jeremy likes you, too.''

''Well, the horses anyway.'' She managed a laugh.

He saw she was on an even keel again. He admired that about the three cousins. They adapted fast. ''Do you have anything that was Bunny's? I'd like to examine—''

''You're still looking for the cause of her death,'' Megan concluded when he stopped abruptly. ''Mother's and Father's things are in their suite. Father wouldn't let anyone bother her things. Grandfather got so upset when I mentioned giving everything to the church charity drive one time, that I've been afraid to bring up the subject again.''

A tingle of intense interest shot through Jess. Maybe there was a clue. ''When can I come up?''

''Tomorrow morning?''

''Good.'' He quelled the need to rush up to the big house at once and start his search.

''I'll introduce you to Grandfather. You can have

lunch with us. Please don't mention that you want to go through Mother's belongings."

"I won't."

The screen door slammed. Jeremy came down the steps, the little girl at his heels. "Want to catch the ball?" he asked her. He rolled a big red ball across the grass. The youngster grabbed it and threw it back, her face as solemn as a preacher's during prayer.

"A kid shouldn't be afraid to smile," Jess muttered.

"I agree. Kate will be good for her. So will Jeremy," Megan told him, confidence returning to her voice. "Does Kate know about us...that we're kin?"

"I told her yesterday. She found out I was checking the back issues of the paper on your parents and demanded to know why. She's very protective of her family," he added wryly.

"I know. We had better include her in further discussions. She can probably tell you more than I can." She hesitated. "I don't think I can call you Uncle Jess."

"Jess will do. Bunny never mentioned me?"

Megan grimaced, then shrugged. "I'm sorry. I don't remember. I've looked at pictures from birthday parties and things in the past. It's like looking at people I know I've met, but from a long time ago, another life, a life I don't remember at all."

He wondered if he'd find any traces of himself in his sister's personal things. The odd ache hit him again, the need for something more from his past. Here, in this setting, he almost felt as if he didn't exist.

For all practical purposes, until he decided what he was going to do with his life, he supposed he didn't.

Washed up. Has-been. Forgotten.

The words were a red-hot poker burning through to his soul. He forced them aside.

"We'll figure it out," he promised grimly. He wouldn't leave without understanding the facts concerning Bunny's death. That was what he was here for, and that was all.

Chapter Six

After talking to his son, Jess peered in the direction Megan and the boy had taken for their ride. He and his niece had explained the relationship to Jeremy, who had taken the news with a combination of disbelief and delight.

With a guilty pang he admitted a kid needed family. His ex-wife had a sister, but she lived in a small town in Vermont and had only visited once during the years of their marriage. That had been the extent of their family get-togethers.

He shoved the guilt out of sight. He needed to talk to Kate, to tell her how the meeting with Megan went and how Jeremy took the news—

Whoa! He brought himself up short. It wasn't that he *needed* to talk to her; it was just…a courtesy. He was renting her place, had sort of forced himself in, and he'd used it as the home base for his investigation. Not that it was any of her business, except that Megan was her cousin....

He stopped arguing with himself only when he stood on the back stoop. Kate was in the kitchen. He watched for a minute without her knowing he was observing her.

Busy with her task, she didn't look up. With slow, almost hesitant movements she wiped down a high chair. Her complete attention was absorbed by the project. He paused, then opened the screen door. Startled, she looked his way.

Her eyes and nose were red, her cheeks mottled. Her lashes were clumped into spikes around her eyes.

He limped across the room. "You've been crying."

She turned her back to him and clutched the edge of the sink. "It's impolite to enter someone's house without being invited," she said coolly.

"To hell with that," he muttered, taking her arm and pulling her around to face him. "What's wrong?"

She jerked away. "Nothing."

He studied her stubborn expression, then glanced at the chair. "Where's the kid?"

"In bed for a nap."

"Where did this come from?" He indicated the high chair.

"It was here. In the attic," she added as if this explained everything. She kept her eyes averted.

The words sounded reasonable, but something didn't quite make sense to him. "Whose was it?"

Her eyes flicked to his, then away. "It was...no one's. Just a—an old high chair in storage."

The chair had no scratches, no nicks or other signs

of wear from years of use. The soft-golden patina of the oak was unmarred. "It isn't old," he corrected. "It doesn't look as if it has ever been used."

She clenched the back of the chair until her knuckles turned white. He had a feeling she was near tears again.

That confused and bothered him. Kate wasn't a crybaby. She was the nurturer of this outfit. Older than her cousins by six or seven years, she'd looked after them like a hen with two chicks. Something was definitely wrong with this picture.

"What does it matter?" she demanded on a strident note. "It was here, I needed it, so I got it out."

"Right," he said, thinking this through. An explanation, shocking and enlightening, came to mind. "You had a child."

Her mouth opened and she sucked in a deep breath. She shook her head. Her voice, when she spoke, was husky but firm. She was in control once more. "No."

He brushed that aside. "I'll ask one of your cousins."

"All right," she snapped. "I lost a child. I was pregnant, but I lost him. A little boy. At seven months. The high chair was for him, a shower gift from friends the week before. There, those are the facts. Are you satisfied?"

"I'm sorry," he said, comprehending the pain she'd kept so carefully hidden, her tears that tore holes in his defenses.

He could tell her it did no good whatsoever to rant and wail about fate. Nothing could change it or make it go away. He stood there and suddenly wished he could comfort her.

"It doesn't matter." She wiped the back of the chair. "It was all a long time ago. It doesn't matter now."

He was whipped at the despair in her eyes. Without being aware that he was going to, he reached out for her. Enclosing her, stiff and resistant, in his arms, he held her and buried his nose in her sweet-smelling hair.

"If it hurts, it matters," he whispered, knowing this much was true for her and for himself. Only Kate had ever made him admit it.

A tremor ran through her. He held her tighter, wanting to absorb the pain she tried to deny, to make life easy for her.

"Don't," she said.

"Katie," he murmured, needing to hold her for reasons he didn't understand. There was just this terrible desire to share the hurt with this woman.

He felt her tremble again, then slowly the stiffness dissolved from her spine, and she relaxed against him. Her arms crept around his neck, and her breath touched his throat.

"You're right. It does matter," she admitted.

His heart knotted at her concession. She sounded exhausted, like a soldier who'd been on the battlefield too long, who had watched all her comrades go down and felt too much in too short a time until all emotion was exhausted.

When she drew back, he did, too. He gazed into her eyes and for a second saw into her soul. "What happened?"

"I can't talk about it. Not now. Please don't ask." She moved aside and bent to her task once more.

Not ever. That's what she meant. He would have to respect that, but he *would* ask. As soon as he read the newspaper reports of her husband's suicide. He would solve the mystery of Kate Mulholland as well as that of Bunny Vickers Windom before he left the valley.

By the time Amanda woke from her nap, Kate had her composure back. Life went on, she had told her cousins often enough in the face of tragedy. So did hearts that had been bruised and broken.

"Would you like a cookie?" she asked the little girl.

The child stared at her with wary eyes that had seen too much of the worst the world had to offer. She didn't reach for the treat.

Kate laid the cookie on the high-chair tray and busied herself with the pot roast she'd put on for dinner. After adding the carrots and potatoes, she put the lid back on and stared out the window, seeing nothing, feeling vaguely empty.

The sun was casting splinters of light on every grass blade and oak leaf. The air was cooling as a breeze swept down from the mountain. Maybe they would get some much-needed rain tonight. She glanced at the child.

"Let's go outside and play," she said, her voice loud in the silent kitchen.

The girl looked out the door, then back at her, indicating comprehension, but her expression didn't vary.

Kate sighed. This was going to be harder than she had imagined. And she had imagined it would be awful.

Forcing a smile, she lifted the girl from the chair and carried her to the picnic table. Gathering some hollyhocks, she removed a stem from one flower, poked a hole in the end with a toothpick, then stuck the stem of another flower into the hole.

"There, a beautiful lady in her ballroom gown," she told the solemn child, who watched everything she did without a word. "My mother used to make them for me."

She fixed two more hollyhock dolls, then waltzed them around the table top, humming "The Blue Danube" as she did. At last she gave up and placed the three dolls in a triangle.

"This is the fairy princess and these are her two ladies-in-waiting, Shannon and Megan."

With a start she realized she'd cast herself as the fairy princess. Was she waiting for her own Prince Charming to come wake her from an evil spell? She glanced toward the garage apartment, realized what she was doing and looked away, angry with herself for thinking of Jess Fargo.

There was no future for her with a bitter ex-cop, but there was something about him that called to mind all the old fantasies she'd once had. Coming from a happy home, she'd expected to find the same in her marriage. Her parents had loved each other. They had shared life. They had made her feel loved and special.

"Hmm, hmm, hmm," Amanda said in a monotone.

Kate's heart contracted. This child had no such happy memories. She held her breath as the girl reached out a cautious hand and carefully lifted one of the flower ladies and moved it, ever so gently, around the table while humming the first four notes of the waltz over and over.

Lifting the other two flowers, Kate waltzed them around the table with Amanda. When the child stopped, she stopped. The big brown eyes looked expectantly at her.

Kate crinkled her brow, trying to figure out what was wanted. Finally she started, "Once there was a beautiful princess who wanted very much to be like other girls."

She bent the front flower petals down, leaving two sticking up in the back.

"But there was this problem—she had two fairy wings attached to her back. Now they were very beautiful wings, but the other girls at school didn't have any. And they couldn't fly. So she was very careful not to use them in front of her schoolmates."

She made up a story about the fairy princess saving a friend's baby sister who had come to school to visit and had fallen out a window, then everyone thought wings were a very useful thing to have.

At the end of the story Amanda lined the flowers up again, then, humming a tune she made up, she climbed off the picnic bench and found the red ball. She threw it to Kate.

When Amanda sat on the grass, legs spread wide, Kate did, too. They rolled the ball back and forth.

Kate's heart swelled as the youngster smiled when Kate announced it was time to go inside and get ready for dinner.

Jeremy dressed in jeans and a T-shirt after his shower. He'd had a super afternoon, riding with his new cousin on a trail up into the mountains, then helping her feed the horses and muck out the stables when they returned.

He saw Kate and the little girl come out on the porch and sit in the swing. "I'm going downstairs," he told his dad.

His father looked up from the televised news of world happenings and nodded.

His dad didn't much like him hanging around Kate, but heck, she was practically a relative. Like Megan. A good feeling rolled over him. He liked this family better than the one in Texas. That made him feel guilty about his mom and stepdad and Aunt Irina, but that's the way he felt.

Besides, Kate and Megan liked him. His stepfather didn't, and his aunt had told his mom he needed to be disciplined. He never had figured out what he'd done to disturb her.

He headed across the grass to the front porch and the old-fashioned swing. "Hi," he said when he reached the steps.

"Hi, yourself. Join us," Kate invited, as he knew she would.

He leaped up the steps in one bound. To his surprise the kid grinned at him. He grinned back. She stuck her thumb in her mouth and leaned against Kate.

"She smiled," he said like an idiot.

"Yes. It surprised me, too." Kate moved over on the swing so he could sit with them. "She spoke during dinner. She said no when I tried to give her a bite of roast."

He laughed when Kate did. The kid smiled and ducked her head. A warm feeling crept up inside him.

"Did you have a good time this afternoon?" Kate asked.

"Yeah." He told her about the ride and everything.

"You're a big help," Kate commented. "Megan won't know what to do without you when you and your dad leave."

The thought of leaving hit him in the chest like a football thrown too hard. He waited for the spasm to pass before speaking. "Maybe we'll stay, I mean, having relatives...a relative...here and all. Dad doesn't have anyone else, you know."

"No aunts or uncles?"

"Well, I don't think so. I never heard him talk about any. Just his sister, Aunt Bunny. He used to tell me stories of their adventures. She could do everything."

Kate nodded. "She was very capable."

"If we stayed, I could learn all about horses from Meg." He let out a heavy sigh. "Dad probably won't want to, even though he doesn't have a job. He's retired now."

"I see," Kate said.

He thought she really did. She understood a lot of things without a guy having to come right out and say them.

They listened to the crickets for a while. Kate set the swing into motion. After about ten minutes he noticed the kid's eyes were closed.

"Mandy's asleep. Amanda," he corrected.

"Mandy," Kate repeated and looked thoughtful. "I like that. It suits her."

"I called her that this afternoon. She didn't mind."

"She's an agreeable little soul. Other than the roast, she accepts whatever I give her to eat or tell her to do. By the way, thanks for playing ball with her today. That was a big help to me."

Jeremy tried not to feel too proud, but it was hard. Here at the ranch he felt…sort of useful. His cousin had said he was a good worker and a natural with the horses. He thought maybe he'd like to be a jockey or something.

Megan could teach him to train horses. That would be so cool. But he'd need to stay here.

He glanced at the apartment. It wasn't as if his dad had a job to go back to, not a real police job, just working a desk. He'd said he wasn't going to do that. Maybe he could find something to do around here.

"Uh, you think there're any jobs open for a retired cop in town?" he asked, keeping the question casual.

"Why, I don't know," Kate said, sounding surprised. "You'll have to ask Shannon if you're interested."

"It's for my dad. I thought we could like maybe stay here for a while." He felt the heat hit his face.

"Oh." She sounded even more surprised.

"It was a dumb idea," he quickly put in before she could get the idea he really wanted it.

She didn't say anything for a long time. He felt really stupid. Boy, he wouldn't bring that up again.

"You should ask. It can't hurt," she told him in the quiet way she had of taking a person seriously. "It might be good for your father. You could go to school in town. You'd have to take the bus. There's one that comes by the end of the road."

That stuffed feeling invaded his chest again. It all sounded too good to be true. He didn't dare wish for it. "Yeah, maybe I'll check it out."

"I can give you Shannon's number at work and her home."

"Okay. You want me to carry Mandy inside for you?"

"I think I'll hold her a while longer. It's pleasant out here. I'm not ready to go in."

So they sat and watched the stars come out. Jeremy thought the evening was very pleasant. He could hardly wait to call Shannon in the morning and ask her about a job for his dad.

Jess asked for Shannon Bannock at the front desk. The police sergeant looked him over, then punched in a number on the telephone intercom. "Go on in. First door on the right," the sarge informed him after a brief conversation with Shannon.

He did as instructed.

"Hi, come in and have a seat," Shannon greeted him. "I've been expecting you."

Her smile was bright, emphasizing the gloominess he personally felt this Monday morning. "I want the police reports on Bunny's accident. Also any information on her husband's death," he said without preamble.

"Yeah, I thought you might." She swiveled her chair around and picked up a clasp envelope. "Here's everything I could find in the files."

He stared at the envelope in surprise when she placed it in his hand. "Thanks. I didn't expect it to be this easy."

"I told the chief about you. He told me to assist you in any way I could, so I dug up everything in the archives yesterday and made copies for you."

It had been Jess's experience that other cops didn't like an outsider messing around in their business. "That was decent of both of you."

"Small towns have some advantages," she said with a knowing grin. "The Windoms have been here a long time. Our great-great-great-grandfather settled in the valley and later told everyone, after the original old-timers had died off, the Wind River was named for him. It wasn't, but such is the conceit of man."

Jess wasn't interested in ancient history, only the past twenty years or so. He itched to get at the reports.

As if reading his mind, Shannon gestured at her desk. "I have work to do. If you have any questions, give me a call and I'll try to find the answers. I'd like to know what happened that day on the lake myself."

"Megan says she doesn't remember anything. Do you?"

Her eyes, blue but with a touch of gray, studied him. He sensed the lively intelligence behind the interest. "Sorry. I can't help you. I was visiting my grandparents on my dad's side of the family when the accident happened. If it was an accident. That's what you're after, isn't it?"

Their eyes met. "Do you think it wasn't?" he asked.

She shrugged. "You tell me." She glanced at the envelope he held. "Maybe you'll find the answer." She hesitated, then asked, "Do you think you might settle around here?"

"And do what?" he asked cynically.

"Oh, a good man can always find something." Her smile took on a devilish tilt. "I heard you were real smart and good at solving crimes."

"Where did you hear that?"

"From Jeremy. He called this morning and wanted to know if we needed some investigative cops."

"He what!"

"Your son seems to think you need a job. Honesty forces me to admit the chief was impressed when I showed him your Houston credentials. Jeremy might be on to something."

"I'll have his hide—"

"No, don't. The phone call was in confidence. I just wanted you to know your son is interested in settling. This would be a good place to raise a boy. He already admires Megan. And he adores Kate. I was wondering how you felt."

A flush hit his neck and crawled upward. Was his attraction to Kate that obvious? "It's none of your business—"

"I meant about living here, not your love life," she added sardonically, her tone mocking his resentment at her prying.

The unexpected and uncalled-for anger subsided. He felt exposed, his nerves on end. "I haven't decided to pull up roots and move. I have a place in Houston."

"An apartment, according to Jeremy. Doesn't sound as if it would be a great hardship to leave."

Her gaze was coolly assessing, the same way Kate sized him up every so often. It put him on the defensive. "I'll think about it. Maybe," he added to let her know he wouldn't be pressured. He stood, the envelope clutched in one hand, and leaned heavily on the cane as he headed for the door.

"Your leg bothering you a lot?" she asked.

"Some."

"There's a doctor in town. Rory Daniels. He might have some advice that would help."

"Thanks." He left the building and hobbled to his truck.

Maybe he would look the doc up. His leg hurt all the time and didn't let up. Spotting a telephone booth, he checked out the doctor's address in the book. Then he noticed the smaller print below the doc's name: Large and Small Animal Clinic.

His eyebrows shot up. The guy was a vet. He chuckled after concluding the recommendation had been Shannon's subtle way of telling him he was a jackass. He'd been called worse.

Sitting in the pickup, he read through the reports Shannon had copied. His sister had drowned. The medical examiner had concluded she'd been unconscious when the boat went down. She'd had a hard blow to the head prior to drowning. Her companion had also been struck by a blunt instrument. He'd had two cracked ribs. His heart punctured, he'd died before the boat sprang a leak and went down.

The last report stunned him. It was about Kate. Her husband had been a Vietnam vet. Jess counted up the years. The man had been seventeen years older than his wife. He finished reading the sparse report, then closed his eyes and leaned his head against the seat.

He had experienced this particular sense of helplessness a month ago. It came from knowing his career was over as, his knee shattered, he'd struggled with the perp. It welled up in him anew, fresh from the bitter spring of despair that knew no solace. This time the feeling wasn't for himself.

"Kate," he murmured and shook his head. The silken threads of shared pain and a lost future wrapped around him, pulling him toward the neat house in the country and the woman who lived there, alone with her awful memories.

Once she'd had dreams, too. Once.

Kate heard the truck's engine on the drive, then the silence when it was turned off. A door slammed. She went to the window and peered out. Jess was standing by the garage and looking toward the house. He was alone.

He'd had a busy morning. Shannon had called and reported on his visit to her office, then Megan had done the same. Jess and Jeremy had eaten lunch at the big house with her and Grandfather. According to Megan, Grandfather had eaten little and had stared at their guests the entire meal, then had gone to his room immediately afterward.

Strange. The older man usually liked company. Although he rarely spoke and writing was a huge chore for him, he would listen to others for hours. When he was alone, he watched TV a lot. Usually he seemed to hate being isolated and rarely went to his room during the day.

She watched Jess as he stared at her through the open window. Finally he walked across the lawn, his limp more pronounced than yesterday. He was supposed to be resting, but she'd seen no signs of that, other than the hour he spent in the sun each day. Otherwise, he seemed to come and go a lot.

Going to the screen door, she held it open while he maneuvered up the steps and into the kitchen.

He looked around, his gaze falling on the high chair. "Where's the kid?"

"Asleep."

He grunted and more or less fell into a chair. His sigh was audible.

"You're not resting enough. Three-year-olds aren't the only ones who need an afternoon nap."

"Don't get bossy."

His words made her furious for a second, then she managed a tight smile. "You're right. What you do is your concern. Except when it touches my family."

"Your cousins are all grown up, too. They don't need a guardian, either."

For some reason his statement made tears burn behind her eyes. She searched blindly in the cupboard for glasses and busied herself pouring tea for each of them. She joined him at the table with the glasses.

He took a long drink. "That hit the spot. It's hot out today. For some reason, I never think of Wyoming as hot."

"We have our moments," she said flippantly.

His gaze locked with hers. Heat surged to her hairline as she realized how that might have sounded.

"Yeah, we do," he said in mocking tones.

"I didn't mean—" She broke off to examine just what she had meant.

"Forget it. You don't have to explain yourself to me."

She sipped the tea and thought of all the times

she'd had to defend herself, her words, her every action. That had been a long time ago. She'd vowed never to live like that again.

"What did you think of Grandfather?" she asked, reverting to her main concern. "How did he take your news?"

"Didn't Megan call and tell you?"

"Some of it. I'd like to hear your version."

"Spoken like a cop," he said, a smile softening his hard features. "He was perturbed when he learned who I was. His hand trembled during the meal. He didn't eat much."

"Yes, Megan thought he was upset and trying not to show it. She said you were going to come back when he goes to the senior citizen's club on Thursday."

"She's agreed to let me go through Bunny's things."

"Those rooms should have been cleared out long ago. Maybe Megan and I should do it now."

"Your grandfather won't like it."

She went on the defensive again. "How do you know?"

"A gut reaction. He didn't like me being there. He didn't like the past being brought up."

"It hurts him." She gave him a glare. "Some people have feelings, you know."

His eyebrows rose mockingly. "Meaning I don't," he concluded without anger.

There was a watchfulness about him that set her on edge, as if he knew something he wasn't sharing. She shook off the intuition. "Meaning some tragedies have the ability to hurt long after the event."

"Such as the day you were shot?"

The silence was instant and total. Like the moment after a gunshot. Once again she saw the flash, heard the blast, and then there was silence. With the silence came the hot, hot pain, ripping into her flesh, tearing into her soul.

The earth tilted strangely.

"Kate," came a gruff voice close to her ear. "I'm sorry. I didn't mean to say that."

She was in his arms, her head against his chest. They were both on their knees on the floor. Confused, she leaned her head against his arm and stared at him. "What happened?"

"You fainted."

She shook her head and pulled away. "I've never fainted in my life. Never."

"Okay," he said grimly. "You had a slight dizzy spell."

He rose to his feet and helped her up as if she were an invalid. She tried to push his hands away, but he only held on that much tighter.

"I'm all right. How did you know I'd been shot?"

"Shannon gave me the report. Megan filled in the details." He eased her into the chair and returned to his. "I asked her."

"Why?" She could hardly get the word out.

He shrugged. "You were a mystery I wanted to understand. I wanted to know why my scars bothered you."

She eyed him suspiciously, her mind a whirl of unconnected thoughts. "They don't. Not now." She rubbed her temples. "I didn't faint," she said, "not even when it happened."

He didn't offer her pity. He didn't mouth platitudes. He simply gave her time to gather her crumpled
defenses. Meeting his eyes, she understood. He'd
been through that same moment of terror and disbelief
that this horror could be happening. The pain had
forced him to accept reality just as it had her.

"You live through it second by second," he said,
as if reading her thoughts. "You get over it little by
little."

"But it always hurts," she whispered.

"Yeah, it always hurts."

Their eyes met and a bond was forged. She didn't
know what it meant—if anything—only that it was
there, not exactly like the intense physical awareness
that had sprang into being that first morning in the
apartment, but that was part of it.

Flames leaped into his eyes, blinding her to all else
but them and the moment. His hands rubbed lightly
on her shoulders, an unconscious gesture on his part.
His compassion was a natural part of him, although
he would deny it if she said as much. The pain of
remembering eased a little.

She let herself lean against his sturdy frame. "You
comfort me," she said, letting the tenderness take her
into forbidden zones.

A quick shake of his head warned her not to go
there.

She smiled, feeling the sadness, but also the delight
of sexual tension, humming through her blood. Closing her eyes, she lifted her mouth to his. His lips came
down on hers.

He took the kiss deep and hard, as if he would
satisfy the hunger they generated on the spot. Her

ready response fed the need, both the physical one and the other, the one that made her want to run, far and fast. Him, too, she thought.

Neither of them retreated, though. Not until they heard the patter of bare feet in the hall did they step back.

"It would be so easy," he murmured. "Too easy."

"Yes," she said, understanding him exactly in that moment.

Chapter Seven

Kate felt like a sneaky thief when she and Jess arrived at the big house on Thursday. They had waited for Megan's call before coming up. Grandfather had gone to his weekly meeting at the Golden Age Club, driven to town by a neighboring rancher, a widow who was close to his age.

"Tell me why I feel so guilty about this," Megan said to Kate when they were inside.

"I feel the same," Kate admitted.

"Would you like some coffee before we start?" her cousin asked, including both of them in the question.

"Maybe later," Jess said.

Megan drew an audible breath. "Well then, let's go." She led the way up the steps and along the hall to the two-room suite at the end of the wing. Her hand trembled when she pushed the door open.

"The room is clean," the detective said with a frown.

"We have a housekeeping service a couple of times a year," Kate explained. "Megan can't keep up the place by herself. All the rooms were dusted and aired a month or so ago."

"Hmm," Jess said.

Megan looked at Kate. Kate shrugged. She had no idea what he was thinking. She glanced around with interest. It had been years since she'd been in this part of the house.

Counting back—she'd been twenty-four when Uncle Sean had wrapped himself around the bridge support—she realized nine years, almost ten, had passed since the tragedy. She'd been deep in her own troubles by that time.

She watched in surprise as Jess walked through the sitting room and straight into the bedroom. She and Megan glanced at each other, then followed. Kate entered the room while Megan lingered in the doorway. Jess went to the bed and checked under the mattress, then looked in the drawer of the bedside table. He withdrew a Bible.

"Sue Anne Windom," he read from the inscription page.

"Dad and I gave it to her for Christmas one year," Megan said. "She wanted a newer version…"

Kate felt her cousin's pain as the younger woman turned from the detective and stared at the portrait of her mother that hung above the fireplace in the sitting room, her eyes filled with emotion. Kate vaguely recalled when the painting was done.

Grandfather had been angry at the cost, but Uncle

Sean had ignored him for once and done as he wished. Aunt Bunny had been radiant at the time, her long flowing gown doing nothing to disguise her advanced state of pregnancy.

"She's beautiful, isn't she?" she murmured to Megan. It wasn't really a question.

Her cousin nodded, her auburn waves gleaming like embers, the same as her mother's hair in the portrait. The artist had captured the banked fire in the thick tresses perfectly.

The opening lines of a classic story came to mind. "Happy families are all alike, but unhappy ones..."

Had Aunt Bunny been another Anna Karenina, unhappy in her marriage and seeking a way out of it?

A chill hit her as another thought intruded. Had Uncle Sean caught her with her lover and, in a rage, killed them both? Had he then committed suicide by driving himself into a bridge five years later, unable to live with the guilt?

But Uncle Sean hadn't been a violent man. He'd been a quiet person, kind to her as a child, showing her magic tricks with a coin. He'd been so happy when he brought his bride home.

Kate turned her attention to Jess. He was methodically going through the bedroom, looking in every drawer and behind every piece of furniture, including the pictures on the walls.

"Let's go get that coffee," she suggested to Megan. "We'll bring you a cup," she said to Jess.

He nodded and continued, totally absorbed in the task.

"He's very thorough," Megan said as they went

down the steps and into the kitchen. She wore a troubled expression.

"Yes. It's his job."

Megan put on a fresh pot of coffee to brew. "Sometimes I've felt so strange when I've looked at Mother's portrait. It's almost as if I can see into her mind. She was unhappy."

Kate nodded in sympathy as Megan broke off and stared out the window at the cattle in the meadow. Kate looked outside.

The grass was lush, irrigated by a creek that ran across the field and meandered into the lake. The sun was shining, lending a harsh brightness to the land. A smaller bird harried a young hawk sailing overhead.

"I want to remember her, but I can't," Megan continued. She rubbed her temples. "Is it that I'm afraid?" She gave Kate a haunted glance. "What happened that day?"

Kate sighed. "I don't know. I don't think anyone does. Or ever will. No one was there to see events unfold."

"No one *alive* at the present. Unless I was," Megan said slowly, pressing the heels of her hands against her eyes. "Perhaps it was too awful for an eleven-year-old to remember."

"Your father didn't kill your mother, if that's what you're thinking," Kate assured her cousin. "He was too gentle, too kind and caring. He loved her very much."

Megan flashed Kate a look of gratitude. "Yes, he did. He would never have hurt her. Never!"

Kate nodded and poured the fresh coffee into mugs.

She set two mugs on the kitchen table. "Stay here. I'll take this to Jess and be back in a moment."

She left Megan and returned up the steps. Jess was in the bedroom closet, a huge walk-in that Uncle Sean had had put in after he and his new wife had taken over the suite. The bedroom on the other side of the closet had become the nursery. Kate herself had rocked Megan to sleep in there many times.

Kate had enjoyed sitting with her cousin. It had made her feel needed, as if she, too, were an important member of the family. She had always been fascinated by babies, whether they were humans, calves, foals, kittens or puppies.

Sure that Amanda was safe in the country setting, Kate had hired Jeremy to watch Mandy while she and his father were at the big house. The youngster was great with the little girl. He let her explore but kept her out of trouble. He played games with her on her level.

Kate wished he were her son.

A giant hand squeezed her heart. Her own child would have been four this summer. Jeremy would have been a wonderful older brother for the son she should have had....

It was foolish to entertain such fantasies. Next she'd be thinking she and Jess and the two kids would make a perfect family. Setting the mug down on a reading table by an easy chair in the bedroom, she mentally shied from the picture thus invoked and the emptiness of unfulfilled dreams.

"Coffee," she called.

Jess stuck his head out of the closet, looked at her

and the steaming mug, then smiled. "Great." He crossed the room and settled in the chair.

"Have you found anything interesting?" she asked.

He sipped the coffee, then held the cup wrapped between his big hands. Gentle hands, she recalled, then glanced away, feeling cold and achy inside.

"Not yet. It's odd," he murmured, "to look at clothes she wore and not know how she looked in them, or what occasions she wore the formal gowns to."

"She and Uncle Sean went to important functions in the state. Before her death he was thinking of running for the state legislature."

"They were involved in politics? What party? Who were his political friends, or, more important, who were his enemies?"

His questions were fired rapidly, the cop on the trail of a clue.

"Your sister's death wasn't a political thing."

His eyes narrowed. "How do you know?"

"There would have been some speculation about it, don't you think? Mr. Burleson would have mentioned it to you. He and his cronies know everything that goes on in the whole state."

"Yeah, you're right about that. I might ask them about it anyway."

She took that as a warning he intended to follow up on this slender lead. He was a persistent man. "Uncle Sean went to college with the governor's son," she told him. "The governor used to come to the ranch to hunt each fall."

Jess considered this information. His sister had run

in affluent circles after her marriage. Putting aside his own faith in her integrity, he considered how she had attracted the rich young rancher and enticed him into marriage. "Did she love your uncle?" he asked.

Kate looked startled. The idea of people marrying without love was obviously foreign to her. She must have loved her husband very much.... And look what it had gotten her, he finished the thought cynically.

Love, or whatever you wanted to call it, was a stupid emotion to fall into. He'd once believed in it. He'd learned better. Kate apparently hadn't.

"I always assumed so," she finally said.

"She might have married him for money." He knew this wasn't true as soon as he voiced the thought. Bunny was as idealistic as Kate.

"I don't think so." She paused. "Aunt Bunny showed me your picture once. She said she'd lost touch with you. She worried about you, more so after she had Megan. She said she used to tell you stories and pretend happier times would come again. But they never did, did they?"

Tears filmed Kate's eyes. Jess tried to ignore them. He'd never met such a tenderhearted person. It bothered him. "Don't take things so hard," he advised harshly. "You'll just end up breaking your heart over and over. That's stupid."

She gazed at him a long moment as if she could see into his heart and was counting each crack and bruise there.

Without another word she rummaged in a bookcase he hadn't yet had time to search. She pulled out an album and flipped through the pages. "There." She gently put the album into his hands and walked out.

He reluctantly looked at the open page. A picture of his youthful self looked directly at the camera. He was in a Little League uniform, his bat over his shoulder. Bunny had signed him up and taken him to practice sessions. She'd attended nearly every game in spite of working part-time at a fast-food place and keeping up with her schoolwork. She'd been the best sister a kid could ask for.

A harsh need to weep hit him in the chest. It had taken him five years after she left before he could cry. That was when his mother had died. He'd wept for both of them. His father had gotten drunk and beaten him for it. His dad had called him a baby and a spoiled brat for showing his grief.

He blinked away the hot, salty burn of tears. It was too late for grieving. Life was what it was. He wished he knew how to make it different.

Why? he questioned. The answers flooded in.

For his son, who sometimes had such hope in his eyes.

For the little girl at Kate's place, who had to hide from her father the way he had often had to hide from his.

For Kate, who had lost her husband and child and yet could find compassion in her heart.

And perhaps for himself, who couldn't.

Kate wasn't sure what was wrong, but Jess was different during lunch. They ate on the back patio. Megan had prepared Chinese chicken salad for them. Kate had brought a cantaloupe and a strawberry pie.

"Were Bunny and Jimmy Herriot lovers?" Jess asked in musing tones, his eyes on the distant peaks.

Kate glanced at Megan. Her cousin sighed and told Jess, "Not that I remember."

"If they were, it wasn't common gossip," Kate added. "I would surely have heard about it."

"Most kids don't know what's going on outside their own little world," he said.

"Kate would have. She took care of all of us." Megan lightly touched Kate's hand, then settled back in her chair.

Kate met the keen scrutiny of Jess's gaze. "There was someone," she said slowly, "someone who might know."

"Who?" he demanded.

Kate glanced at Megan, then back to Jess. "Kyle Herriot. He's the son of Jimmy, the man who was killed with Aunt Bunny."

"Why would he know anything?"

"He was the last person to see them alive," Megan explained. "He saw his father and my mother on the boat dock that day. He said they seemed upset, so he didn't bother them."

"There was no mention of that in the police report."

There was a moment of silence. Finally Kate said, "He was a boy, eleven at the time, I think. It was his father who was dead. Why would his name be in the report?"

"Because he was an eyewitness. If there was foul play—" Jess stopped abruptly and glared at her.

Kate drew a slow, careful breath. "You think they were murdered," she concluded.

"It wasn't my father," Megan stated with fierce uncertainty. "Someone else did it."

Kate stared at Megan in surprise. It appeared her cousin, like Jess, had also thought of foul play regarding the deaths. Until today, *she* hadn't.

Jess studied Megan without speaking.

"He wouldn't!" Megan insisted.

"Of course he wouldn't," Kate said, putting in her two cents' worth. Jess turned those all-seeing eyes on her. Her defenses slipped and she felt bared to the soul-searching gaze.

Later she spoke about it again. "You're wrong about Uncle Sean," she said on the silent trip back to her house. They were in Jess's pickup.

"Am I?"

His tone bothered her. It told of a cop who'd seen too much of the underbelly of the world, who no longer took anything on faith or at face value.

Maybe she should learn to be more like him, she mused. Maybe life would be easier that way. Actually her life had been on an even keel before Jess and his son showed up. She'd been happy, well, content, with things at that point. Now she found herself thinking constantly of a family...of *them*.

She sighed, then smiled at the foolish pictures that came to mind, and felt as forlorn as the little match girl in the fairy tale.

When they stopped beside the garage, Jeremy and Mandy raced each other across the grass toward them. The long-legged youngster let his charge stay ahead.

"Your son is a wonderful person," Kate murmured before climbing out.

"Yeah. You probably wonder how, having a parent like me, he could have gotten that way."

She rounded the truck and stopped beside him

while he retrieved his cane from behind the seat. "You are not the only person in the world who ever had a hard time. Stop feeling sorry for yourself and start counting your blessings. Jeremy's one of them." She marched off toward the racing youngsters.

Kneeling in the grass, she impulsively opened her arms when the laughing duo neared her. Mandy flung herself against Kate's breast and rested, her face flushed and alight with triumph at winning.

"Well, looks as if you two have been having a good time," she commented lightly, rising and heading for the house with the child cuddled against her.

"We weeded the garden," Jeremy told her. "Uh, you won't have many radishes this year. We, uh, thought they were weeds until I noticed the little radishes on the roots."

Kate laughed and told him how she pulled up a whole row of sweet corn when she was a kid, thinking it was wild grass. "Did you guys eat the lunch I left?"

"She ate all of hers and wanted part of mine," he complained good-naturedly.

"Wow, you must have been a hungry girl," she said to Mandy, making her eyes big and impressed.

"Do you think your cousin needs any help with the horses this afternoon?" Jeremy asked as they went into the kitchen.

"Call and ask. Here, let me pay you for baby-sitting."

"That's okay. She wasn't much trouble."

Kate smiled at the description. "Nope, a deal's a deal." She figured up the amount and handed it over after setting Mandy in the high chair. ''Thanks for the help.''

After he left, jumping off the steps into the grass in a single bound, she gave Mandy a cup of milk and two cookies, then put her down for a nap in the room that had served as a guest bedroom and her mother's sewing room when she'd been Mandy's age. She tossed a load of towels into the washer, cleaned the bathrooms, then went out on the porch with a glass of tea and a magazine.

Jess was on the deck over the garage. He'd changed to shorts and was sunning his legs. A pang went through her as she recalled the scars on his knee. What would he do with his life now that he could no longer be quite so active?

He would tell her it was none of her business. And he'd be right. She sternly opened the magazine and read it from cover to cover. Or started to. Her eyelids drooped. Nabbing a pillow from the chair, she stretched out on the swing, one foot on the porch in order to keep up the soothing motion. She finished an article and started another. She didn't get to the end before she was asleep.

Kate woke to the step-thump of her renter on the porch. She sat up and blinked at him, the afternoon sun causing her to squint sleepily.

He stopped a couple of feet away. ''There's something restful about a sleeping woman,'' he murmured, his gaze dark and moody. He didn't look at all restful, but more like a hungry lion on the prowl.

Her blood thrummed pleasantly through her body. She was hungry, too. She wanted the feel and smell and taste of him. She wanted to bury her face against his chest and know his strength surrounded her, tempered by the gentleness of his care for her. She wanted too much, she reminded herself.

"Is there something you need?" she asked when he continued to gaze at her. "Towels? Sheets?"

His lips curled into an attractive half smile. "The perfect landlady," he mocked, but with a gentleness at odds with the hunger in his eyes.

She dropped her gaze. Her hands were clenched in her lap. She unlocked them and smoothed her hair into place. "What do you want?"

"Do you have a motor for the rowboat? It's made to take one on the back."

"I think there's a trolling motor somewhere in the garage. Kris liked to cruise around the lake, supposedly fishing but mostly staying out of the way of 'honey-do' projects."

He laughed, surprising her.

She laughed, too, and was surprised again, this time at herself.

"That's the first time I've heard you say his name," Jess said, his manner thoughtful.

"But you knew it. Did you read the newspaper accounts? Of course you did," she answered her own question.

"How did you get to the phone to call for help? You had to have been bleeding badly."

"I crawled," she said. "How did you get the guy who shot you and was trying to take a woman hostage?"

"Mostly hopped on one foot." His smile was like

a lost ray of sunshine beaming on her. "We're a matched pair of warriors."

"Scars and all," she said, agreeing.

"Someday you'll show me yours," he said in a deepened voice, low and sexy and thrilling.

She tried to shake her head, to deny the hunger, but she couldn't. His eyes locked with hers. Messages sped between them like golden sparks bouncing from her to him, him to her.

"The motor?" he finally said.

She led the way to the garage. Together they searched through boxes she should have thrown out long ago and along shelves piled with broken parts to equipment long discarded.

"My gosh, the clutter," she grumbled at one point.

He grunted and continued searching through a big box of odds and ends. After ten minutes, they found the motor on a shelf mounted over the garage door.

"It doesn't look too promising," she ventured.

He took the small engine outside to examine it. "I think I can clean it up and get it running. If you don't mind."

"Of course not. Are you going to fish?"

"I'm going to cruise around the lake," was all he would admit to.

"I know generally where the sailboat went down. I can guide you there," she volunteered. "That's what you want to know, isn't it?"

"Yes." He laid the motor on the picnic table. "Does that bother you?"

"Lots of things about you bother me, but your investigation isn't one of them."

He sucked in a sharp breath. "You don't pull punches," he muttered and reached for her.

She came willingly. He hauled her up tight against him. She gripped him just as hard. Their kiss was deep, hot and satisfying. He slanted his head first on one side, then the other as they tried to absorb the full taste of each other.

She moaned as the need raged furiously through her and arched against his strength. His hands slid down her body and cupped her hips, then her buttocks, letting her feel the full force of his hunger for her.

"This isn't enough," he growled, biting at her lips, then soothing them with little flicks of his tongue. He lifted his head and looked around. "Come upstairs with me."

"I can't. Not now." She kissed his chin, his jaw, his neck, wherever she could reach.

He exhaled a harsh breath. "When?" He gripped her hips when she moved against him and held her still.

"I don't know. Maybe never." Her thoughts were disjointed, but she knew they were on fragile ground...one step either way, and they would be lost....

"Don't say never," he whispered, his mouth at her ear, nibbling, sucking, giving pleasure.

She could feel his heart beating against her breasts and see the fast pounding of his blood in the measured tick of a pulsing artery in his neck. Inside, heat wove magic threads of pleasure to the innermost parts of her. And yes, it wasn't enough. She, too, wanted more.

Fulfillment. The filling of her senses with this man. The merging of their bodies in sweet ecstasy. The finding of total bliss. Yes.

A tremor raced over her. His arms tightened.

"I dream of you," he said, an accusation in the words.

"I dream, too. Dreams aren't any good—"

"Reality is better," he agreed.

"—because they never come true."

"This one can and will," he told her fiercely. He kissed down her neck and licked the valley between her breasts.

Focusing on her cotton shirt, his eyes were hot and consuming. He slipped his hands under the material and cupped her breasts. Her nipples were hard, aching points. He made them ache more by brushing his thumbs over them again and again.

When he opened her shirt, then his, she watched breathlessly as he brought his lips to one pebbled tip. He used his tongue and lips expertly, driving her before the gale force of desire. When she rubbed against him, he shuddered and breathed deeply, quickly, as if reaching for control that was fast speeding past his grip.

"I've never wanted a woman this much," he said, almost as if he accused her of unfair play on his senses.

"I know. I didn't know what it was to be this *hot.*"

"Yeah, hot," he agreed, moving against her so that waves of pleasure rebounded through her. "Gotta sit, or we're both going to end up in the grass."

She laughed softly and felt his chuckle against her belly. He turned them and sat on the edge of the table.

She leaned into him, her thighs clasped securely between his.

"Oh-oh," he murmured. "We have company."

She jerked around. Mandy stood at the screen door, her solemn gaze on them. When she saw Kate looking at her, she smiled, her hesitation obvious.

Kate pushed away from Jess. The afternoon breeze rushed around her body, cooling her to sanity once more. She smiled at the child. "Hi, come out and play," she invited.

"We'll finish our game later," Jess murmured, his fingers busy at his shirt buttons.

She glanced down and quickly refastened and smoothed her own clothing. "How about helping me bring out some cookies and milk? Jess is thirsty," she called to Mandy, who was clambering down the steps.

"He's hungry," he corrected in a low growl at her back.

She laughed and ran to Mandy. Taking the little girl's hand, she led the way inside and prepared a glass of milk and two of tea. "Here, can you carry the cookies?"

Mandy nodded, her eyes bright and trusting. Kate's heart did a hitch. Outside, once more at the picnic table, but much more circumspectly this time, the three of them ate peanut butter cookies and talked about going for a cruise on the lake when Jess got the motor oiled and gassed up.

"Boat," said Mandy, pointing out on the lake.

A sailboat rode before the wind, its canvas brilliant stripes of yellow shading into gold, red-orange and red.

"That's Kyle Herriot," Kate told Jess. "He often sails on the lake. Shall I invite him over?"

"Yes," he said.

The green eyes were watchful, assessing. The hard-boiled detective was back; the eager lover was gone.

She retrieved a flag from the garage and stuck it in a holder on a dock post. Reality had indeed returned.

Chapter Eight

"Kyle, this is Jess Fargo," Kate made the introduction. "Jess is a detective from Houston. Bunny Windom was his half sister."

"Glad to meet you," Kyle said. "I've heard about you from the old-timers in town. Tom Burleson says you're investigating your sister's death."

There was curiosity in Kyle's dark eyes and a certain wariness, which was natural. After all, Jess was asking a lot of questions about two deaths that had been ruled accidental.

"I've been piecing together the details," Jess explained in an easy manner.

"Have a seat, Kyle," she invited. "Mandy and I'll bring some iced tea out. Want to come help?" she asked the child.

Mandy nodded. Kate tossed a smile toward the men

and held out her hand for Mandy. Her gaze flicked to Jess before she walked away. Her heart did a double take.

His eyes reflected a yearning and a hopelessness so deep it made her tremble. The yearning was replaced by bitterness, hiding the other emotions and ushering in the harsh, cynical facade he used so effectively.

She understood he used the cynicism as a barricade to hide his more vulnerable self, just as she used the ranch and her home as a refuge to hide from others. The reclusive widow, as Shannon called her. Life was easier this way.

Mandy took her hand, bringing her out of the odd moment of introspection. They went inside and left the two men alone.

Kate took longer than necessary to prepare a glass of tea for their latest guest. Watching from the kitchen window, she saw Jess talk earnestly to Kyle. Kyle frowned and shook his head. Jess persisted, his gaze intent as he questioned the younger man. She could see that Kyle was becoming angry. Jess looked even more fierce as he probed deeper into the mystery.

Kyle stood abruptly.

She figured it was time to intervene. "Come on, sweetie. We need to get outside before the men come to blows."

Mandy brought along the plush bunny Kate had found in the attic when she'd searched for the high chair. She had also moved the toys and children's books she'd collected during her pregnancy to the guest room where Mandy slept.

Both men were silent when she set a frosty glass in front of Kyle. She found the red ball and asked

Mandy if she'd like to play. The child promptly sat on the ground, once again her legs spread wide, so they could roll the ball to each other. Kate joined Mandy on the ground.

"So?" she said, glancing at the two men who looked like gladiators carved from stone. "Are you two going to be enemies instead of working together to solve the case, assuming there is a case to be solved?"

Jess gave her a frown what would have fried eggs at thirty paces.

Kyle relaxed. "You always did come straight to the point," he said, smiling slightly.

"I see no reason not to." She grinned at him, then frowned at Jess. "Lighten up, Detective. Glaring doesn't win friends and influence people."

"Huh," was his moody reply.

"I take it Kyle doesn't remember anything helpful," she said to Jess, then in an aside to Kyle, she added, "He hates to be thwarted."

"There's nothing much to remember," Kyle told her. "Dad was taking the sailing sloop on a check-out run. She'd had some damage to the hull during the storm the week before. I was mad because he wouldn't let me go. I followed him down to the marina, but he'd already sailed. He returned to the dock, but before I could get my courage up to ask again if I could go out with him, I saw Mrs. Windom aboard the sloop."

Kate nodded. "She liked being out on the lake."

"I could see she was upset," Kyle continued, "so I stayed hidden behind the storage shed. She and Dad talked. She was crying. It looked like a bad situation. I decided to skedaddle. I went home. That's it.''

Kate nodded and rolled the ball to Mandy. ''Good catch,'' she said when the child grabbed the ball.

''My dad and your sister were not involved in an affair.'' Kyle ended his tale with a heated glare in Jess's direction.

''That's what I told him. Nothing can stay hidden in a small town, especially clandestine meetings. Someone always sees and reports the couple,'' Kate said, also directing a chiding glance at Kyle, then catching the ball Mandy rolled back to her.

''Your faith in the efficacy of the gossip mill is reassuring,'' Jess said, mocking both of them. His expression changed, becoming intense again and serious. ''This is an isolated area. There are four ranches plus National Forest land that border the lake. The Windom ranch claims the longest stretch of shoreline, the National Forest property is second, the Herriot place third. The two smaller ranches between the Windoms and Herriots are owned by a doctor in town and Kate's former mother-in-law, who lives with her daughter in Colorado.''

''What are you getting at?'' Kyle demanded.

''What if someone joined Bunny and your father? What if there was a fight and Bunny and Jim Herriot ended up dead? What if the perpetrator then sailed the boat out on the lake and scuttled it? Since no one saw him, there's no one to say what happened to them and the boat.''

''Uncle Sean wouldn't have killed Bunny,'' Kate insisted.

Jess snorted. "Passion crimes are unpredictable. The mildest of men can be pushed too far."

Mandy ignored the ball when it rolled between her legs and stared at the adults, her big brown eyes wary as she looked from one to the other.

"It's okay, Mandy," Kate assured the girl. "We're just talking. No one is mad."

Kyle stood. "Thanks for the tea. I've got work to do, so I'll shove off."

"What kind of work?" Jess wanted to know.

Kyle frowned in annoyance, then shrugged. "I run a three-thousand-acre ranch. I raise cows, horses, hay and sugar beets. We own the ranch supply store in town."

"And about half the buildings on Main Street," Kate added.

"Actually, five buildings," Jess said without inflection. He named the stores. "Is that correct?"

A muscle ticked in Kyle's jaw. "Yeah."

"I checked out everyone bordering the lake. If that makes you feel any better," Jess explained.

Kyle shook his head. "Cops," he said, and walked off.

Kate was enchanted when Jess smiled—sardonically, of course—and joined Kyle down at the dock. His smile erased some of the harsh cynicism of the tough cop and softened his oft-times somber expression.

A fluttery feeling settled around her heart. Jess and his son would be gone at the end of the month, she reminded herself. Twelve more days. He had arrived on June fourth. Ten days ago. For some reason she felt as if she had known him forever. He warmed the cold spots within her.

Mandy picked up the ball and threw it. "Catch," she called out.

Kate barely had time to throw her hands up and grab the ball before it hit her in the face. "Wow, good throw. We'll sign you on with the Yankees."

Mandy scrambled to her feet and dashed toward the garden. "Shoo, shoo," she yelled.

Kate laughed when three crows took off for dear life. They settled in a walnut tree and cawed irritably at the humans.

Jess came up the garden path.

"Jeremy must have taught Mandy to watch for crows in the garden. She's better than a scarecrow. I'll have to hire her," Kate confided.

He slumped down on the bench and watched Mandy, who was now chasing a butterfly. He rubbed his knee.

"Do you want an ice pack for your leg?" Kate asked, sensing the pain he tried to ignore.

"No."

She clamped her teeth together. So much for feeling sympathy for him. She wouldn't offer him another thing for the rest of the month—

"I'm sorry, Kate," he said softly. "I'm frustrated and taking it out on you. Kyle Herriot was my last hope for discovering something new on the case."

"Perhaps it's time for you to put the past behind you," she suggested in a carefully neutral tone as she watched Mandy play at the edge of the garden.

The little girl, so sweet and good-natured it made Kate's heart knot up, kept looking at them every little while, as if to make sure they were still there. She ached for a child who had learned such fear in her short life.

"I don't need a guidance counselor," he informed her, bitter and cynical once more.

"Well, pardon me." She got to her feet, determined to leave the grouchy bear alone in his misery.

He, too, stood. "Don't go," he said softly, the words strained, as if he really didn't want to say them but had to.

She rounded on him, angry and not sure why. "I don't need this. I don't want any complications in my life. And I don't give a damn what you do with yours."

"Liar," he murmured, stepping close.

To her surprise he nuzzled his face against her temple and into her hair. Little whorls of excitement eddied through her, at the same time a knot of tears formed in her throat.

"Katie," he said on a low groan of agony. "You make me want to dream again. Tell me not to be stupid."

"Don't be stupid."

He sighed and slipped his arms around her waist. They stood there for a minute like that, not speaking, while need and hopelessness formed a dark aura around them.

"Sometimes," she whispered, "sometimes I don't understand myself."

"It's a mystery," he agreed. "But this part is simple."

He lifted a hand to her face and stroked her cheek with the gentlest touch. She really felt she needed a good cry. The need increased at the tender but sad smile that played briefly at the corners of his mouth.

"We want each other. That's as old as time, as elemental as the ground we stand on. It's the other things that make it complicated."

"What other things?" she asked when he laid both hands on her shoulders, his thumbs rubbing soothing circles on her collarbones.

"I don't know names for them," he admitted. "Part of it is your goodness. Shannon described you well. You're like the earth—a nurturer."

His voice dropped so low she had to strain to hear him. She didn't dare move.

"I want that part of you, too," he said. "And that scares me. I don't want to need anyone that way or that much. It makes me think of commitment and forever. But I know better. I'll never let that happen."

"Jess..." She couldn't find a coherent thought among the confusing riot in her mind, in her heart.

"I'm leaving, either at the end of the month or shortly thereafter. When I'm satisfied I have the facts of Bunny's death or that I can't go any further. I mean that. No matter what happens between us."

Kate checked on Mandy, who was pulling hollyhock flowers off the stalks, then looked at Jess. "Be careful, Detective," she warned. "You already have one crack in your armor. Your son. You're not as tough as you pretend."

"Don't go thinking you'll change things, that somehow we'll end up one big happy family. I don't want you on my conscience when I leave."

She smiled at the irony in that. "You don't have

to worry about me. I've never entertained any fantasies about us.''

She knew that for a lie as soon as she said it. Some stubborn part of her still hoped, still wished, still dreamed of finding the perfect love….

Meeting Jess's sharp gaze, she knew he realized it, too.

But she also saw what he kept so defiantly hidden. ''You want the same things,'' she said softly.

''I don't believe in fairy tales.''

''But you still have dreams. Everyone does. That's no sin.''

''It's foolish,'' he said, the bitterness increasing in his voice and his eyes. ''It's foolish, Kate.''

Again his voice dropped. She felt anguish, his or hers she wasn't sure, only that it was real and that, behind it, hope pressed against the barriers each of them had erected against future hurt.

''Wouldn't it be nice if we could go back in time and find ourselves the way we were…once…a long time ago?''

''I was never as young and idealistic as I think you must have been. My father had a way of forcing reality on a person.''

Impulsively she hugged him close. ''Poor lonely boy,'' she said, not at all mockingly.

He held her off with hands that were no longer gentle, although he didn't hurt her. ''I don't take pity or charity from anyone. Not ever.''

''I know.'' She sighed, feeling the moment slipping away and missing the closeness of sharing old hurts and memories. She sat on the picnic bench and watched Mandy as she tired to make flower ladies.

"You're doing great with your son. He's at ease and happy now, more so than when you arrived."

Jess picked up his cane but didn't leave. "You and Megan and Shannon treated him like a friend from the first. Now you accept him as part of your family."

"He's a good person. We've all fallen in love with him."

"He likes Megan and Shannon. He's mad about you."

She smiled at the steely tone as Jess admitted his son's feelings. He hated to give an inch in this battle he'd decided existed between them. That his son liked her and her family he had to concede.

"And that's dangerous to your peace of mind," she murmured.

"Correction. *You're* dangerous to my peace of mind."

She swung toward him, her heart beating wildly. His gaze was as passionate as his tone had been.

"Yeah," he said as if she'd questioned him. "You make me dream. You make me want. Even though I know happily-ever-after is a lie. I'm not going down that road again."

He walked off, anger in his stiff back and a determination to get away from her. The problem was she knew exactly what he meant. Passion could be a treacherous path. It could lead to wild, unfulfilled longing. And neither of them wanted that.

"Oh, it's too hot to do any more today," Kate announced, removing her gardening gloves. She and Jeremy and Mandy were weeding and spreading new mulch around the plants. "Let's take a break."

''Maybe we can go for a swim in the lake,'' Jeremy suggested, wiping sweat off his face on his sleeve.

She considered. ''Good idea.'' She caught Mandy up and swung her high over her head. ''Want to go swimming?''

''Yes, want to go.''

''Meet you at the dock in five minutes,'' she told Jeremy, who loped off toward the apartment to change.

In her bedroom she slipped into her old one-piece suit. It had been years since she'd worn it. A shiver ran over her. The last time she'd worn a bathing suit, she and Kris had had a fight about it.

She sighed. She needed to take her own advice and put the past behind her. ''Okay, Kate is ready. Let's see what we can do for a suit for Mandy, okay?''

Mandy nodded.

Kate had noticed the child never used the pronoun *I* or referred to herself in any manner. Worried that she had no firm sense of identity, Kate had taken to referring to herself and Mandy by their names.

''Let's take your shorts and top off. You can swim in your panties and, umm, how about this T-shirt?'' She held up one of Mandy's faded shirts. ''Does Mandy want to swim in this?''

''Yes, please.''

The child had manners. Her mother, whatever her problems, had taught her daughter to be polite. Kate spared a moment of deepest sympathy for the young woman who had thrown her life away and left this precious little human without protection and care. In that instant Kate knew she wanted to adopt Mandy.

She bit her lip to stop its trembling as she realized

the implications of taking in a child, of opening her heart to love and the hurt that could come with loving. She sighed, knowing it was too late. She already loved this sweet little girl who observed the world with her big, brown and wary eyes.

After changing Mandy, they walked down the garden path to the lake.

"Last one in is a drooly dork," Jeremy called, racing past her and Mandy.

Mandy let go of her hand and ran after the youngster. At the dock Jeremy lifted Mandy high in his arms, told her to "hold your breath" and jumped in.

Kate smiled at Mandy's squeal of laughter as the cool water rushed over them and up to their necks. She sat on the dock and eased into the lake, then swam a few strokes to loosen up. Once, she had brought Megan and Shannon down here nearly every summer day. She'd taught them to swim and row and sail just as her mother had taught her.

"Let's teach Mandy to swim," she called to Jeremy. "Show her how to hold her breath and go underwater and open her eyes first."

He was at once interested. She liked that about him—his curiosity and keen intelligence, qualities she was sure he had gotten from his father.

They spent the next hour doing preswimming exercises.

"How come you know all this stuff?" Jeremy asked once they were sitting on the dock, resting and drying in the sun before going back to the house.

"I had a lifeguard course in high school. I gave swimming lessons at the community pool in the summer while I was in college."

"Far out."

She smiled at the expression. Slang seemed to repeat itself every few years. "Far out" and "way cool" had been expressions her group had used. A sense of nostalgia rolled over her, but it was gentle instead of harsh. There had been many good times in her life, much more than the bad.

Jess tapped the ballpoint pen on the table at the diner. "One more question," he said to Shannon.

She glanced at her watch. "Okay. I still have a few minutes before I have to meet with the D.A. Fridays are always hectic at the department," she added, and sighed.

"What was Kate's marriage like?"

His question took the local law officer by surprise. She caught her breath, then let it out in a whoosh. "You don't ask for much."

"The basics. Was it happy at first? What went wrong?"

"Well, I was fifteen when they married, but I don't recall a lot. The wedding took place in the garden at Katie's house. Kris was seventeen years older than she was."

Jess nodded. "I saw that in the newspaper account of his death. Why did she marry him?"

"I think she felt sorry for him. He grew up on the ranch next to Kate's place. He was so lost after he came back from Vietnam. His father had died. His mother had closed up the house and went to live with her daughter. He came back to…nothing."

"He was listed as a rancher. Was he?"

"He tried, but his family place was too small to

make a living. Kate was fresh out of college. She came home and took over the ranch books for Grandfather and Uncle Sean. She also took on some of the local businesses, friends from school who asked her. Not too many. She prefers her garden to anything else. Bookkeeping is for cash flow.''

''I figured as much. You were right. She is reclusive.''

Shannon nodded, her expression thoughtful. ''When she loves, it's total. She gives her all. She hides at the ranch in hopes of not getting involved with people. I don't think that's good for anyone.''

''Kris was diagnosed with post-traumatic stress disorder, according to the newspaper.''

''Yes. It was scary. I saw him one time when he…regressed, or whatever you call it. He and Kate had taken me and Megan for a hike up to a ridge for a picnic. On the way back, he suddenly ducked behind a tree and told us all to get down. I thought he saw a bear or something.''

Jess nodded impatiently, wanting her to go on.

''Then he said the Cong were coming, that they would soon have us surrounded and we had to slip away. He led the way off the trail.'' She sighed. ''We all got poison ivy. It was the most miserable two weeks I'd ever spent.''

''Was that the first time he acted that way?''

''I don't know, but it wasn't the last. He seemed to get worse. Kate got him to go to the veterans' hospital. They ran some tests, including psychiatric evaluation, gave him some pills and sent him home. I don't think he ever took the pills. I know he never went back for help. He got worse as time went on.

He accused Kate of running around on him. He called her a slut and other names if she even spoke to a male friend. It must have been very embarrassing for her.''

"Why didn't she leave him?"

"It's hard to walk out, especially when the other person is sick. Besides, Windoms don't give up easily. My mom should have left my father before their first wedding anniversary.'' She made a gesture as if sweeping that memory aside and continued with the other couple. "Besides, Kris was wonderful, except when he was crazy.''

Jess felt a pang deep in his gut. He realized he'd wanted her marriage to be miserable and recognized the inherent selfishness of the thought. Did he picture himself as her knight in shining armor? Ha!

Shannon reminisced. "He was funny and gentle. He'd been an Eagle Scout and knew everything about the woods. Megan and I visited their house a lot as kids. He and Kate always made us feel welcome. Kris showed us how to live off the land if we needed to. When he went off the deep end, he always worried about Kate and us girls. He thought we were in danger from the Vietcong and would make us hide.''

"So why did he shoot her?"

"I think he got confused. His spells of lucidity were growing less and less frequent. His accusations grew wilder. At the same time, he was afraid for her and the baby. He told her the Cong would rip her open and kill the baby. That last day he was outside with a gun, holding them off and yelling for her to take cover. She tried to talk him down. A mistake, that. She said he was horrified when he realized he'd shot her.''

"So he killed himself in remorse," Jess concluded.

"Kate thinks so, and I have to agree."

He heaved a sigh. The slow winding-down of his marriage seemed trivial next to the trauma Kate had suffered. No wonder she didn't want complications....

He paused at the thought. *He* certainly didn't intend to become one of the problems in her life. He knew better than to think they could make it, two wounded souls seeking solace and solitude. No, it would never work.

"I've got to run," Shannon said, rising.

"Thanks for the information. I was curious."

She gave him an assessing glance that brought the blood to his ears. "Were you now?"

"Yeah," he replied gruffly, feeling exposed.

She smiled, told him goodbye and hurried out. He paid the bill and walked slowly to his pickup, the tap-tap of his cane underscoring all the reasons he should get out of town. Out of the state. It was time he thought about starting home. Houston. That's where he meant, not the five-thousand-acre Windraven ranch.

When he arrived at Kate's, he found the apartment and the house empty. He spotted Jeremy and Kate and Mandy down at the lake. They looked happy and preoccupied with their endeavors. Yeah, a Norman Rockwell painting come to life.

But for some reason, cynicism didn't block the pain in his heart this time, or block out the longing for something more from life.

Kate helped Mandy build a sand castle of sorts on the shore of the lake. The beach was equal parts mud, rocks and sand. Jeremy was innovative at using all three components.

"Here's Dad," he said in surprise.

Kate was at once aware of her state of dress. Or undress, as the case actually was. Her bathing suit was one piece but cut high on the legs. It felt too revealing.

"Looks like you guys are having fun," Jess said, joining them and sitting on the dock with his feet in the water.

She glanced his way. He had changed from the dress slacks and white summer shirt he'd worn when he left for town that morning. Now he was in a pair of cutoffs and an old T-shirt with the word *Pig* barely visible. She supposed he didn't mind the insulting nickname for a policeman.

His legs were long, lean and deeply tanned from his daily sunning. He possessed a sinewy strength, a steadiness in his gaze and a ready-for-anything composure that were very appealing. Her heart did its clenching act.

When she realized he was looking her over in the same assessing manner, she looked away, aware of his scrutiny the whole time she and the two kids worked on the castle. At last Jeremy pronounced the project done.

"It's time to go in," she said. "Mandy and I need a bath before we prepare dinner."

"I bought hamburger and buns," Jess said. "I thought Jeremy and I would treat you to a meal. If you don't mind my using the grill."

"Of course not." She realized she might have

agreed to eat with him. "But you don't have to invite us—"

"I know we don't have to," he said. "We want to. Don't we, Jer?"

"Sure." Jeremy looked from his dad to her and back again, clearly puzzled at undercurrents he didn't understand.

"Okay," Kate agreed uneasily. "What time shall Mandy and I be ready?"

"Is six too early?"

"No. That's fine. Let's go," she said to Mandy. "It's time we got all cleaned up." With that she made as graceful an exit as she could, wishing she'd brought towels down to the dock.

At the house she gave Mandy a bath, then let her watch a *Magic School Bus* video while she took a quick shower. After pinning her hair back at each side, she went to the kitchen to see what she had to contribute to the al fresco meal.

She looked down at her slacks and fresh white cotton shirt. This outfit wouldn't bring the flames to any man's eyes. A shiver ran over her as she recalled the heat in Jess's eyes when he'd taken in her bathing suit. Perhaps she should shop for a new one, one less provocative.

No. She was letting the past interfere with the present. She'd done nothing wrong. Besides, she'd liked having his eyes on her, male appreciation and attraction in those forest-green depths.

It came to her that she was beginning to enjoy being a woman again, that it really was all right for a man and woman to smile and tease and flirt, to be attracted to each other, even if nothing would ever come of it.

A flicker of sadness passed through her. She sighed, then laughed ruefully at the mocking twists of fate. She and Jess were a lot alike—two dreamers who had once thought they could right all the wrongs in the world.

And then they'd learned they couldn't.

Chapter Nine

Kate glanced out the window to check on Mandy, who had gone outside when Jeremy and his father had come down from the apartment. Mandy watched, seemingly content to be near her hero while the men worked on the boat motor at the picnic table.

After folding the last towel in the dryer, Kate laid it on a fluffy stack. She'd washed sheets and towels first thing that morning and scrubbed the two bathrooms, then ran the vacuum when Mandy woke up. There was only the dusting left to do.

If things worked as planned, the four of them were going to have lunch down on the dock and take a cruise around the lake afterward. If the motor worked.

She worried about their lives becoming more entangled. Last night Jess and Jeremy had cooked hamburgers on the grill, and they had eaten outside. The two men had done everything, including serving a dessert of ice cream and sugar wafers. Both father and son had been at ease, taking her ribbing about the burned buns with pretend outraged male pride and lots of quips about whose fault it had been.

They had continued talking and laughing while the sun went down and the moon came up. At nine she had taken a sleepy Mandy inside and put her to bed, breaking up the party. It had been a nice day, she'd concluded when she went to bed.

A part of her longed to go outside now and repeat the camaraderie. No good could come of such longing, she reminded herself. Summer dreams. Where would they go when winter came?

She put the towels away and doggedly did the dusting. Outside she heard Jeremy call to Mandy. He told her they were ready and to get Kate.

"Okay," Mandy called back. "Please come. Jeremy is ready," the little girl told her, her nose pressed against the screen.

"Be right there." She put the dust cloth away, grabbed a hat, a shirt and the sunscreen and headed out.

"Does it work?" she asked the men, eyeing the motor. The small boat engine looked brand-new. Every part gleamed.

"O ye of little faith," Jess groused. "Of course it works. Didn't you hear it running?"

"Well, I think I heard it sputtering once," she said with a straight face.

Jess gave the motor to his son. "Carry this down to the boat. I'll bring the tools. We'll mount it on the transom while the girls get the meal laid out."

"Come on, Mandy," Kate said, holding out her hand. "We've been given orders. Let's get the lunch."

All four of them gathered on the dock ten minutes later. She and Mandy opened the picnic basket and served sandwiches and chips. There was lemonade for everyone. By the time she called, "Ready," the men were finished.

Jess sat down and stretched his injured leg out in the sun. "Ahh," he murmured, "it feels good to sit."

"You're doing too much, Dad," Jeremy advised him. "The doc said you were to do moderate walking and resistance training, but you're not to stand or do chores any length of time."

Jess frowned severely at his son, but his voice was good-natured when he spoke to Kate and Mandy. "Remind me not to take this nag with me for any more checkups. He recalls every word the doctor said…and reminds me of each and every one of them daily."

Jeremy grinned and, leaning against the post, wolfed down one sandwich and started on another. Kate noticed the father ate heartily, too. The chips and salsa soon disappeared.

"Now for the pièce de résistance," she announced and removed a bowl of sliced strawberries and four shortcakes from the basket. She divided the treat into four bowls and had Mandy hand them around the group.

"These are the best strawberries I ever ate," Jeremy declared after taking a bite.

"They're the ones you and Mandy picked yesterday. They are good, aren't they?"

"They are," Jess agreed.

She saw his chest lift and fall in a deeply drawn breath. He looked…contented. A strange word to apply to this restless man, but it fitted. At the moment.

His son looked happy, too. Jeremy had eaten the dessert and was teasing Mandy by pretending to steal a strawberry from her bowl.

It's good for her here, Kate thought. She glanced at the two males, both basking in the sun and looking very pleased with the day. The ranch was good for all of them.

Turning her gaze to the mountains, she fought off longing and loneliness and other undefined emotions. Four years ago she'd accepted the fact that she wasn't destined to have a family of her own. But she'd vowed at the time she would be the best "honorary" aunt any kids ever had when Shannon and Meggie married and had their children.

Packing up the basket, she admitted she was thinking quite seriously of a family of her own again. If she adopted Mandy…if the court would let her keep this sweet vulnerable child, she would be the best mother she could.

And if the judge said no?

Then she would have had this moment of happiness to tuck away into her heart. She paused, surprised. Yes, she was happy, the frigid emptiness of her life full at the moment. It seemed so odd, like getting a gift for no reason.

Jess pushed to his feet. "Well, son, shall we take the boat out for a test run?"

"Sure. Uh, Kate, you and Mandy coming?"

She realized the youngster liked having her and

Mandy along. They acted as a buffer between him and his dad. During the time they'd been in the apartment, the relationship between father and son had become easier for each of them. They were doing things together now and enjoying it.

However, time was running out. There were only ten more days before the end of the month. The two men would be heading back to their real lives in Houston then.

Without letting herself dwell on this fact, she shook her head in response to the invitation. "Mandy and I don't want to get stuck out on the lake and have to row in. You two do the test run. We'll join you if it's a success."

"Let's show the ladies we know a thing or two about making repairs," Jess said to his son.

With that, he led the way onto the fishing boat and cranked up the engine. Jeremy untied the line and pushed off.

"Bye," Mandy yelled at them. "Be in by dark."

Again Kate had to laugh at the advice delivered in a very grown-up manner. She wondered if Mandy was repeating her mother's orders to her and if the little girl had been allowed outside for hours at a time without supervision.

Some kids had to grow up early, she mused. Jeremy and Mandy were examples. And Jess.

When the men returned, she and Mandy joined them. They rode around the lake for most of the afternoon, exploring its nooks and crannies and observing the ranches around its shore.

"Look, a fox," Jeremy said, pointing.

A red fox lifted its muzzle from the water and

stared at them. It decided they were no threat and finished its drink. It trotted off into the National Forest land with its tail streaming out behind it.

"You can tell a fox from a coyote at a distance by the way they hold their tails when they run," she told Jeremy. "Foxes hold their tails straight out behind them. Coyotes run with their tails tucked between their legs."

"Neat," he said. "Did you see the fox, Mandy?"

"Yes. And the babies."

"Babies? There weren't any babies," Jeremy corrected.

"There are three kits playing at the edge of the woods," Jess said softly. "Look."

Kate looked back at the spot where the fox had disappeared. Sure enough three little ones peeked over a log in their direction, all eyes and pointy ears.

"Pretty," Mandy said. "I want one."

"They are darling," Kate agreed. "But they're wild animals, Mandy. They have to stay with their mommy and learn to live in the woods. We'll have to see about getting us a kitten or a puppy."

"Why not one of each?" Jeremy suggested with a grin.

Kate thought that sounded fine. She'd grown up with dogs and cats as well as cows and horses. Her eyes met Jess's. He gave her a curious look. She realized she was planning a future and Mandy was already part of it.

"Complications," he murmured, a wry smile playing around his mouth.

But his eyes...those sad, sad eyes. She looked away with an effort.

* * *

Kate set Mandy on the day bed in the guest room. "Now let's say our nighty-night prayers."

Mandy bowed her head, put her hands together under her chin and closed her eyes. They went through the "Now I lay me down to sleep" prayer together.

Kate bent over to kiss the little girl good-night as she had every night since Mandy's arrival last Sunday. Today was Saturday. A week. It seemed like a lifetime, as if this sweet child had been part of her life forever.

To her surprise Mandy threw her arms around Kate's neck and hugged her tightly. "I want to stay here," she whispered as if fearful to say the words aloud. "I want Jeremy to stay. And Jess. We can all live here with you."

Her heart in her throat, Kate swallowed twice before she could speak. "I would love for you to live here with me. I'll ask Officer Shannon about it. We have to go to a judge and ask him or her if it's okay, though, to make it all legal."

"Like adopt-son?" Mandy asked wistfully.

Kate experienced the quick smart of tears. "Yes, like that."

Mandy's mouth turned down sorrowfully. "Do girls ever get adopt-soned?" she asked anxiously.

Kate tried to figure out exactly what Mandy was asking. "Of course. If the judge lets me adopt you, I'll be your mommy and you'll be my daughter. We would be a family."

Mandy looked skeptical and woebegone. "Two boys got adopt-soned. They said girls couldn't 'cause only boys could be sons."

"Oh, honey," Kate said, finally catching on to Mandy's worry. "It's adopt-shun, not son. It means, um, the process of adopting someone, whether a boy or girl."

"I want to be your little girl." Mandy released her hold on Kate. "My mommy died. She said someone would come and get me, but she didn't know who. She said not to cry or no one would want me."

Kate realized the mother must have known she was dying and had tried to prepare her daughter. Her heart ached for the woman and the sorrow she must have felt.

"It's okay to cry when you're sad, Mandy. Everyone cries then, even grown-ups."

"Do you cry?"

"Sometimes. My mommy died, too. It made me very sad. I cried then. So did my daddy."

Mandy relaxed with a yawn. "I cried once, but the lady said not to."

"What lady?"

"The policeman came and gotted me. He gave me to the lady. She didn't want me, but the policeman said she had to take me. She had two other kids. The boys got adopt-*shunned*."

Kate busily smoothed the covers while she fought back an overwhelming grief for what this innocent little girl had gone through. She wished she could have a word with the "lady" who had forced a little girl to bottle up her sorrow for fear of being rejected.

"Well, I'm glad Officer Shannon brought you here. I have plenty of room." She nuzzled Mandy in the tummy with her nose, bringing a giggle from the girl. "Especially for a neat person like you."

Mandy turned on her side and stuck her thumb in her mouth. "Will we get a puppy?" she wanted to know. She yawned again.

"Definitely. As soon as the judge says you can live here all the time."

The soft-brown eyes closed.

Kate sat there on the side of bed, watching the little girl sink into sleep, the worried frown now gone from her young face, her entire manner one of trust.

God help me, Kate issued a silent prayer. She would rather die than disappoint this child. Bending, she kissed the smooth cheek, then tiptoed out of the room.

Shannon was waiting at the house when Kate and Mandy arrived home from church the next day. Although her cousin smiled at her and stooped down to tell Mandy how pretty she looked in her yellow dress, Kate detected the frown that tightened the lines around the other woman's eyes.

"Stay and have lunch with us," she invited.

"Can't. Got to get back. I'm on city patrol this afternoon. One of the guys called in sick today."

Kate led the way inside the house which was blessedly cool compared to the ninety-five degrees in the sun. She'd closed the windows and the curtains before leaving for church.

"Mandy, let me unbutton your dress, then can you go to your room and change to a pair of shorts and a top?"

"Sure," Mandy said, sounding very much like Jeremy.

Shannon smiled slightly at the eagerness of the

child to please, then, when Mandy had left the kitchen, turned to Kate. "Bad news."

"What?"

"Mandy's father has been spotted. He was identified by a deputy in the next county at a gas station."

"Did they arrest him?"

"No. The deputy called for backup. Ray Collins must have realized he'd been spotted. He took off, then abandoned the car, which was stolen, at a strip mall on the outskirts of the next town, and, we think, hitchhiked out of town."

"So that's what has you so worried."

Shannon flashed Kate an apologetic look. "He's headed this way. His wife finished school here in town. He must have figured out she came back to these parts."

"I see," Kate murmured, thinking of his threat against Mandy.

"There's more," Shannon continued. "A pawnshop was broken into a couple of days ago. His fingerprints were identified in the place. So we know he's armed."

"Armed and dangerous." Kate shook her head. "Why would he want to kill his daughter?"

"I don't know. I've come to take her—"

"What?"

"I've arranged another place for her to stay. A deputy, a female one, on leave from the sheriff's department for a rest, said she'd take Mandy until we capture Collins."

"No."

"Kate—"

"We can't just shuffle that child around like a bag

of potatoes, storing her this place or that. It isn't right.''

Shannon pressed a thumb and finger across the bridge of her nose. ''I know, but the situation is bad. I think Collins will kill anyone who crosses him. I can't put you in that kind of danger.''

''I've been there before,'' Kate reminded her.

Shannon sighed and looked at her helplessly. ''I know. That's what bothers me. I thought the state police would have this guy locked away again by now. He's slipped through all the roadblocks. He's crazy and crafty and determined.''

''I can't let her go,'' Kate said softly but adamantly. ''I want to adopt her.''

''Oh, Kate.''

''Mandy needs a home. I have one to offer. Is adoption possible?''

''I don't know. The father is the complication. I don't know if the court would decide we had to have his consent, since he's the child's parent or if a convicted felon loses all rights over his child's fate.''

''I have Jess Fargo here. He's a cop. He'll help if I need him. Besides, Mandy's father doesn't know she's at my place, does he?''

Shannon shook her head. ''But he's smart. He could ask around. You were at church with Mandy this morning, so lots of people know where she is.''

''If you feel she's in greater danger here, then of course she should go, but if not...if you're moving her because of danger to me, don't. I'll be careful from now on.''

''Don't bring her with you if you come into town,'' Shannon advised. ''Keep her out of sight as much as possible. We have an all-points bulletin out on Collins. He'll be spotted if he shows up in these parts."

Kate relaxed. Mandy was staying with her. "I have an automatic pistol Kris bought for me to use. In case the enemy soldiers showed up. I know how to fire it."

"Are you licensed?"

"Yes."

"Okay. Someone from the sheriff's office will be patrolling the county road out here twenty-four hours a day from now on. I need to talk to Jess, too."

"He's up at Megan's with Jeremy."

"Okay. Tell him to call me when he gets in."

"I will. Can't you take five minutes for lunch?"

"No. I have to get back to town. Be careful. If you see anything at all suspicious or that makes you feel uneasy, call me or the sheriff's office. We'll check it out."

Kate nodded, a frisson sweeping along her spine at the thought of a possible killer lurking around the ranch. Mandy returned to the kitchen before Shannon got out the door.

"Say goodbye to Shannon, Mandy," Kate said in cheerful tones. "She has to go back to work while Mandy and Kate get to play and weed the flowers all afternoon."

Mandy giggled at this news and told Shannon goodbye. Shannon gave her a kiss on the cheek, then peered intently at Kate. "Don't be heroic," she ordered.

"Don't worry. I'm not going to do anything stupid."

After Shannon left, she and Mandy ate lunch, then

read two books before it was time for the youngster's nap. Kate read the Sunday paper, entered the monthly bills for the ranch on the computer bookkeeping system, then rested on the sofa after making sure all the doors were locked.

Maybe it was a good idea to keep the house locked all the time until Mandy's father was in custody again. She would talk to Jess about security. With the tough cop in residence, she was sure they would be safe. On this thought she dozed off.

It was nine that night before Kate heard his truck on the gravel driveway. She breathed a sigh of relief. She'd been tense all afternoon, imagining a sinister shadow behind every bush as she and Mandy gathered vegetables, weeded the flower beds and later watched minnows swimming in the shallows around the lake. The youngster had been cheerful and seemingly unaware of the tension that crawled along Kate's neck.

"Jess," she called softly from the front porch.

He paused beside the truck, then turned her way and walked over to the steps. "Yeah?"

"I need to talk to you. It's about Mandy," she added quickly, in case he got other ideas.

"What about her?"

"Her father was spotted near here—in the next county, actually—but presumably heading this way. Shannon says he's armed. He intends to kill Mandy, then himself, according to some of the inmates at the state prison."

"When the hell did you find this out?"

"I knew from the first. Shannon didn't think about

the guy heading this way. He supposedly didn't know where his wife and child were living.''

Jess grimaced. "A guy in prison can find out just about anything if he's patient and tries hard enough.''

"Well, he seems to know Mandy is somewhere around here. Or maybe he thought of Wind River because his wife went to school here her senior year while her father worked at one of the ranches for a while before moving on. They lived a sort of vagabond life, I understand.''

He climbed the steps. "Let's go in. I need to sit down. Then you can tell me the whole story.''

In the kitchen she put on a pot of coffee and sliced two pieces of chocolate cake. She joined him at the table when the coffee was ready. "I don't know much else. The mother was on some kind of drug. She apparently got hold of a bad dose and died recently.''

Jess muttered a raw expletive. "We do this to ourselves," he said in a rough voice. "Human weakness. It's a wonder we've survived this long.''

"It's what we do to children that bothers me," Kate told him. "How do I protect Mandy? How do I watch for her father? I have a .38 automatic.''

He gave her a narrow-eyed scrutiny, then said, "Let me see it.''

She went to a picture on the wall, found the catch that opened it, then removed the gun from the wall safe and handed it over. She shut the safe and returned the picture, a scene depicting a mountain storm, to its place.

"Kris?" Jess asked, pointing toward the safe.

"Yes, he put it in. He wanted me to have protection in case I needed it when he wasn't available.''

"From the Cong."

"Yes."

Jess shook his head. "You've had your share of weirdos—" He broke off. "Sorry."

She managed a smile. "Kris did go off the deep end. I don't deny that."

Jess examined the weapon. "The gun is in good shape. Clean and oiled. Do you have bullets?"

She rose and went to a drawer of odds and ends. She pulled the box from the back of the drawer and took it to Jess.

"Let's see you break the gun apart," he ordered.

She did so.

"Okay, put it back together and load it."

Without allowing herself to feel anything, she quickly put the parts together and the bullets into the clip. She left the firing chamber empty.

"Good. You do that like a pro."

"Kris insisted I practice." She wiped their fingerprints off the gleaming metal and laid it on the place mat.

"You had better start carrying it," he advised. "Do you have any kind of holster?"

She nodded. "A shoulder one. You really think I need to wear it?"

"As long as this guy is on the loose, yes."

"Everyone is looking for him. His picture was on the news this evening. He surely can't get far before he's—"

"You don't know the criminal mind," Jess broke in. "Never assume a perp is going to give up until he lays the gun down and puts his hands up. Then be doubly careful."

"Is that what happened to you?"

"Yeah. He was hiding in an alley behind a Dumpster. He told me he was coming out and not to shoot. I had him toss his gun out first. He had another one. He came out shooting."

"You were lucky it was only your knee. It could have been worse."

"Yeah," he said bitterly. "I could be dead. Instead I'm a crippled ex-cop. A wash-out."

A bitter silence fell between them. Unable to stop, she slowly rose and went to stand behind him.

"Don't hand me pity. I don't want it."

"I know." She laid her hands on his shoulders. The muscles were coiled like steel springs. A pulse hammered in his throat, giving away his suppressed anger and despair. She knew both emotions well.

She rubbed until the tension dissolved somewhat from his body. Bending, she planted a gentle kiss on the top of his head, the way she might have done with Mandy if the child had suffered a scrape.

The chair skidded back as he stood, taking her by surprise. He rounded on her. Then she was in his arms.

"Do you know this?" he snarled at her. "Do you know how much I want your touch? And that I want to touch you." His hands pulled her solidly against his tall, strong frame. "In every way," he added softly, hoarsely. "In all the ways there are. You're all the good things—the ones I always wanted."

She barely had time to draw a breath before his mouth was on hers, hot, hungry and desperate. She wrapped her arms around him and returned the kiss, as needy as he.

The heat was instant, surrounding her with desires that hadn't been fully fed in years and years. She moaned slightly and knew all her barriers had been breached in the instant he reached for her. The kiss went on and on.

At last he drew back, his gaze hooded, his face cast in stone as he watched her.

"I won't say no," she murmured. "Not tonight. If you want to leave, do it now."

"Jeremy's spending the night at Megan's. There's nothing to go home to."

She understood what he meant. There was nothing at the apartment to make him think, to draw him away from this madness. "Mandy sleeps all night."

"Then it was meant to be," he said with a sardonic half smile, half grimace of despair.

She never knew who reached out first. They were standing apart, then they weren't. Their bodies merged as naturally as a sea gliding onto a shore. They kissed again. She loved the way his hands caressed along her back, the way his lips and tongue sought hers, the way his thighs opened to let her step closer.

The embrace seemed right, as if the moment belonged to them, only to them. She wanted to breach the barriers of clothing and past hurts and fearful emotions until there was nothing between them but pure consuming passion. They kissed and caressed and strained closer for long, mind-drugging minutes. Finally, with a shudder, he drew back slightly.

"The bedroom?" he asked, his lips sending showers of hot sparks down her neck to lodge deep in her chest.

"Yes. Upstairs."

He let her go, except for a hand on her waist. "I hope you're not waiting for me to carry you."

His tone was teasing, and she laughed, not expecting humor from him. When she met his eyes, a tremor ran through her. He was smiling, too, but his eyes were intense, aflame with the fires they had generated between them.

Silently they walked to her bedroom. She closed and locked the door behind them, flicking the switch. The room became filled with the light from the bedside lamp. He sat in a chair and removed his shoes. She turned back the covers on the bed.

Her fingers went to her blouse. She hesitated. Going to the bathroom, she turned on the nightlight she kept in there and partially closed the door. Then she turned off the lamp. The bedroom dimmed into soft shadows. Better.

When she started back toward the bed, he caught her wrist and pulled her into the space between his thighs. "Let me," he said. "I've dreamed of this often enough."

He unfastened the blouse and slipped it from her shoulders. He yanked his T-shirt over his head and dropped it behind him in the chair. He continued to remove a piece of her clothing, then one of his, until they stood face-to-face with nothing between them but air.

Together they climbed into bed. A breeze stirred the curtain as the cool mountain air flowed into the bedroom, but nothing could chill the fire that blazed between them.

Propped up on one arm, he explored her body by

touch, cupping her breasts, one, then the other. The light seemed to pool in his dark eyes, giving them a soft glow as he followed the trail of his fingers along her abdomen. His hand stilled when he came to the first scar.

He circled the indentation caused by shotgun pellets fired at close range, his eyes riveted to the spot an inch to the side and slightly down from her navel.

"Why did you approach a man with a loaded gun?" he asked.

"I'd always been able to talk him down before."

"But not this time."

"No, not this time."

To her surprise he bent and kissed the spot with the gentlest of touches. "I'm sorry, Katie," he murmured.

She stroked her hands through his hair. "It's okay. I've learned to live with it."

He lifted his head, his eyes locking with hers. In his she saw pain, a brief flare of sadness so deep it reached all the way to his soul. She realized the pain was for her.

She stroked down his strong body until she touched him intimately. When she looked again, the urgent flames of desire had superseded the sadness. She smiled at him, happy they were together, that they could give each other this moment. Thoughts faded as their kisses became all consuming.

"I don't have any protection, but I'm clean," he assured her at one breathless point. "I went a little crazy after the divorce, but I had tests after that. I'm okay."

She lightly caressed his lean cheeks, his jaw and throat. "So am I."

"Then what are we waiting for?"

She saw the teasing light was back in his eyes. She liked that. She tickled him in the ribs, then flung a leg over his thigh. He groaned as she rubbed playfully against him.

"You'll pay for that, woman," he warned, then branded her with hot kisses along her throat and down to her breasts.

They were perfectly suited to each other, she realized as they kissed again. Both had been wounded, physically and emotionally. Both were cautious of passion and the sense of commitment that could accompany its fulfillment. They were each hesitant to become this involved again.

But the moment was too compelling, the sharing too urgent to regret this one night of appeasing the hunger and the need.

"Tomorrow," she whispered as his hands sought her in intimate caresses. Tomorrow would be time for regrets. She touched him every way she knew to bring him to pleasure.

"We'll worry about it when the sun comes up," he whispered, echoing her sentiments.

"I'll pray the dawn never arrives." She knew when he became still that she had given away more than she meant to, perhaps had made an admission to feelings she couldn't, wouldn't, name, not even to herself.

"So will I," he murmured and thrust gently into her. "Ah, Katie," he said. "You feel...like paradise."

She let the passion take her, and it was more demanding and more fulfilling than she'd ever experienced. He was passionate and tender and so very, very careful with her. It almost made her weep. Later she did. A little.

He held her close. ''It'll be okay,'' he told her, pulling the sheet over their heated bodies as the mountain wind grew colder. ''It'll be okay.''

He sounded hesitant, but the words contained a vow. She hugged him, an impulsive act of closeness rather than passion. ''I know. We'll both be okay. Tomorrow will be fine.''

''Tomorrow,'' he echoed, doubt buried deep within the word.

But she felt the promise of it like the soft light of the summer sun creeping over the horizon. She snuggled against him and went to sleep.

Chapter Ten

Jess awoke with the dawn. A smooth bottom was pressed against his side. Without considering the action, he turned and cupped his body around Kate's and pressed his face into the wild tangle of dark hair with its fiery highlights. It had been years since he'd awakened with a woman in his bed.

Her bed, he corrected, and knew a second of total and unexpected bliss. Inhaling deeply he relived the hot passion of the night, the sweetness of her mouth, the warm invitation of her body as she'd accepted him as her lover. It had been heaven. And now, after the passion, hell.

He would be leaving in a few days, returning to his real life. Right…the empty apartment he'd lived in for the past few years. Some life.

Fate always had the last laugh. First it had taunted

him with the knowledge that there were good fathers, ones who played with their kids and loved them and taught them happy things about living. He'd known that from Bunny's stories of her dad. Next it had given him a son, a tiny being who had filled his heart to the bursting point…and then had taken him away, except for every other weekend and two short, harried weeks in summer.

Jess no longer considered his ex-wife among his blessings, although he had during the first years of their marriage.

Having a wife and a place of his own to come home to had been the all-American dream for him. But his ex had wanted more—more money, more time, more prestige. When he'd turned down an offer to head up security for a big company after solving a case for them, his wife had told him to leave. So much for marriage.

He stroked Kate's shoulder and felt heat surge from his innermost being to all parts of his body. Finding this woman was the ultimate joke on him. What did he, a crippled ex-cop, have to offer her?

Nothing.

The emptiness enclosed his soul and echoed back like the *ping* of a depth finder in an ocean trench.

"Mmm," Kate said, a sleepy, don't-want-to-wake-up groan.

She stretched and yawned, then snuggled against him again, her hand settling on his hip and sending splinters of light through him.

"Stiff?" he asked, putting a smile in his voice as an incredible tenderness came over him. He wanted the morning to be as perfect for her as the night had been for him.

He was certain she hadn't made love with anyone in the years since her marriage had ended in tragedy, just as he hadn't since the six anger-driven months after his divorce. During the night she had been fiercely hungry and sweetly giving, meeting his passion with a gratifying intensity.

"Mmm," she said.

A little, he interpreted. He smiled and nuzzled his nose against her neck, inhaling the warm, womanly scent. It flooded through him, filling him with longing he knew he should ignore.

He didn't or couldn't. He wasn't sure which.

With a low groan he wrapped an arm around her waist and hauled her closer. His need was blatant, but there was nothing he could do about it.

"Someone's come to visit. And so early," she teased, turning over and planting burning kisses along his collarbone.

She was all sweetness and womanly delight. He couldn't get enough of her warmth, her mouth that had touched him everywhere during the night, her need that matched his own.

After a slow, satisfying repeat of the night, they took a quick shower together. She let him use her toothbrush, an act that struck him as so intimate he would have taken her back to bed if they'd had time.

"Mandy should be up soon," she told him, glancing at his body, a smile on her face.

He followed her to the kitchen when they were dressed. They had just finished breakfast when the little girl entered the kitchen, bringing a stuffed toy with her. "Mandy is hungry," she announced.

"Oh, is she?" Kate asked as if shocked at the idea.

With a laugh, she scooped the child into her arms and planted loud kisses on Mandy's cheek and neck. Mandy squealed with laughter.

Jess's heart gave a hitch, then raced as if he'd just come upon a crime scene in the making. He looked away and encountered the puzzled glance of his son through the back door. "Jeremy's home," he said.

Kate set Mandy in the high chair and unlocked the back door. "Jeremy. Come on in. Mandy's about to have breakfast. Would you like to join her?"

The boy came inside, his gaze running from Kate to him and back to Kate. "Uh, I already ate with Megan. What's Mandy going to eat?"

Kate, smiling, set a container of pastries on the counter, then fixed Mandy a bowl of cereal. She poured Jeremy a glass of milk and set it in front of him. "Help yourself. I got these at the bakery Saturday."

The boy needed no further invitation. He picked out the biggest cinnamon bun in the box.

"It looks like rain today," Jess said after a couple of minutes of silence.

"I hope it will. The grass needs a deep soaking." She glanced at Mandy, then back to the window. "Summer showers are usually noisy. The thunder reverberates between the hills and makes an awful racket."

"Is Mandy afraid of storms?" Jeremy asked.

"No," Mandy said, and shook her head emphatically.

Kate smoothed the hair back from the girl's face. Jess's heart squeezed down to the size of a peanut. The gesture had been so natural, as if she'd been taking care of Mandy since birth. He considered how the four of them must look, all gathered around the breakfast table like a family just beginning the new day.

It was never going to happen. He'd gone through those dreams. They'd all been used up a long time ago. Like him.

Feeling sorry for yourself? a part of him mocked.

Yeah. Because it would be so easy to dream again, but he wouldn't. He had no right to dream.

"I've got to go," he announced, standing.

Startled eyes—incredible blue ones, green ones similar to his own and huge brown ones—all turned on him. He felt exposed, vulnerable to the raw, new feelings he couldn't put a name to. He grabbed his cane, propped against the wall, and went out the door as if the hounds of hell were breathing on his heels.

But he knew he wasn't going to outrun the need that gnawed at his heart, making him long for a life that couldn't be.

Crossing the dew-damp grass to the apartment, the wind blew dust into his eyes. From the cottonwoods that lined the creek, he heard the incessant caw of the crows and thought of Kate's tale about them signaling a disaster.

The birds were restless because of the storm, his logical self sneered as a chill attacked his spine.

But which storm, another part of him slyly inquired, the thunderstorm from the mountains or the one inside him?

* * *

Kate heard the engine before she saw the sheriff's four-wheel-drive vehicle come around the curve of the lane. She smiled at its occupant from the porch swing where she rested after working in the garden all morning. After lunch, she'd worked on the ranch books, then on Rory Daniels's receipts from the veterinary office. Now she was waiting for Mandy to wake from her nap.

"Hello, Gene," she called when the sheriff crossed the flagstones to the house. "Did you catch Ray Collins yet?" she asked, hoping that was his news.

"No, there's no sign of the man." Gene bounded up the steps and settled into the rocking chair. "Muggy today."

"Yes, I've thought all day it was going to pour any minute, but the storm keeps holding off."

"Yeah. How's that tenant of yours doing?"

She tensed. Heat crept into her face. She hoped Gene didn't notice. Jess had gone to the apartment when he'd left the three of them in her kitchen. She hadn't seen hide nor hair of him since.

"Fine, I guess. He was around earlier, but I haven't seen him since this morning. Mandy and I worked in the garden."

"You're being careful, aren't you?" Gene demanded.

"I keep a .38 on hand," she admitted.

"I remember that gun. Kris bought it for you, made you get a license and learn to shoot."

"Yes." She watched the dark-gray clouds swirl around the peaks to the west of them. "Jess said I should wear it. I don't, but I keep it on hand."

"You got it now?"

She lifted a cushion on the swing and showed him.

"Good. Keep it handy. I don't like the idea of this Collins fellow being after you."

"After Mandy. Shannon said he intends to kill his daughter, then himself."

Gene sighed heavily. "I don't know what gets into folks. Ah, there's your tenant. Hey, there! Jess!"

Kate swung her gaze toward the garage. Jess made his way down the steps and over to them. He used the cane, but he seemed to be walking easier than he had in days. His limp was hardly noticeable. He gave her one quick but intense glance as he came up the steps.

"Sheriff," he greeted the other man. "What brings you out this way?"

"No good news. Just wanted to check in with Kate here and make sure she was protecting herself."

"I'm keeping an eye out," Jess told him, taking a seat on the top step.

"Good. I wanted to see you, too," Gene continued. "The county needs a forensic man on the force, someone to explore the crime scene before it's messed up by deputies who don't know beans about preserving evidence. They're volunteers. What training they get, I give. An experienced man such as yourself would come in real handy for us."

"Are you offering me a job?" Jess asked, one dark eyebrow lifting up.

Kate could have kicked him for the suspicious tone as well as the sardonic quality in his smile.

"Nope, the county commission would have to approve it first. I just wanted to feel you out, see if you've thought about settling in these parts now that you know you have family here. Wind River isn't as exciting as Houston, but we have our moments. It's a good place to raise a boy.''

Jess's green eyes flashed to Kate. The heat rushed to her face again, stronger this time. Did he think she'd put the sheriff up to mentioning the job possibility? She carefully kept her expression neutral while her heart rate doubled.

Jess looked back at the sheriff. ''I appreciate your thinking about me, but I intend to head back to Houston at the end of the month. I don't see any more leads in my sister's death.''

''I heard you were looking into the accident.'' Gene rubbed his chin and was silent for a minute. ''I was the investigating officer in that case. After the coroner's report of accidental death by drowning, the D.A. decided we didn't have any reason to pursue it further.''

''You didn't see anything when you examined the boat?''

Gene shook his head. ''We didn't actually see it. It went down in the deepest part of the lake, probably a hundred feet deep. Since it was ruled an accident, the department decided not to spend funds to bring in equipment to haul the boat up.''

''Why did the boat go down?''

''Well, we figured Mrs. Windom tried to sail it back to shore after Jim Herriot was injured. Since she wasn't an experienced sailor, we thought she probably turned it over. A diver checked the boat and found a hole in the side. That could have been caused by hitting a rock when it went down.''

The sheriff's story was a bit different from the one

Jess had read in the newspaper, but it was still speculation. No one knew the real facts of the case.

"Funny," he said, "that neither the Herriots nor the Windoms insisted it be brought up. It was an expensive sailboat, wasn't it?"

The sheriff shrugged. "The insurance company paid off. I guess technically it belongs to them. They didn't want to spend more on it, either." He rose. "Well, I'd better go. Keep a sharp eye out. Kate, make sure your doors are locked. Best to keep them locked all the time until we catch Collins."

"I will," she promised.

"One more question," Jess said.

The sheriff nodded and waited.

"In the police report it said my sister had a blow to the head that probably knocked her unconscious. That explains why she drowned when the boat went down. The owner of the boat had a blow to the ribs strong enough to shatter bone. He was dead when the boat went down."

"Yeah, that's right."

"I'm just a city cop, but I'd suspect foul play in a case like that."

Kate glanced quickly at the sheriff to see how he took this implied insult.

He nodded thoughtfully instead of getting angry. "There were rumors, of course," he said. "People thought all kinds of things."

"Such as?" Jess demanded.

"Some thought it was a murder-suicide type of thing—"

"Hard to believe that," Jess broke in. "Did Herriot knock Bunny out, then do himself in by whacking his ribs until one pierced his heart?'' He snorted at the logic in that.

The sheriff continued, ''Others thought Mrs. Windom's husband had caught them together and attacked Herriot, killing the man. He then knocked his wife unconscious and, thinking she was dead, sunk the boat in the deepest part of the lake.''

''And?''

Gene spread his hands. ''And nothing. Out here in the back country, rumor doesn't hack it in a court of law.''

Kate smiled as the sheriff got in a little gibe of his own in the city-cop versus country-cop contest. Jess did, too.

Watching them, she realized the two men liked and respected each other. They talked a few more minutes, then Gene insisted he had to go. She waved when the sheriff drove off. Jess moved to the rocking chair.

''Ah,'' he said, ''that feels better.''

''Is your leg bothering you very much?'' she asked, at once sympathetic. ''Did…was last night…?''

''Making love didn't hurt it,'' he finished for her.

This time she knew the heat showed up as a blush. Her cheeks felt as if they were glowing. She took a careful breath. ''Do you regret last night?''

He was silent so long she thought he wasn't going to answer. ''Nothing could make me regret one of the best experiences of my life,'' he finally said. ''But I'm leaving at the end of this week.''

''That's not quite the end of the month.''

''Yeah, well, it's time I got back to Houston.''

''To what?''

"A desk job, if I want it. Maybe I'll go to college and become a lawyer. I have enough saved up to make it through."

"That's a very good idea."

Jess gave Kate a sharp glance. She looked and sounded sincere. His heart kicked around in his chest. "There's no place for a woman in my life."

Her hands clenched. She clasped them together and folded them in her lap, a ladylike pose that touched something inside him. He wished he'd met her long ago.

"I understand." She gave him one of her dead-level perusals. "I did from the first."

He nodded. "That should be a relief, so why do I feel so damned miserable?"

Kate laughed, surprising him. "Maybe because you're doing what you think you should and not what your heart wants."

"I gave up on that organ a long time ago."

Her beautiful face became pensive. "So did I."

The confession did something to his insides. Her smile was so damn brave it made him angry that she'd been hurt. There was a quietness in her eyes, as if she held herself still, and with it, the sadness he'd noted before. He had to get away from her, or else he'd start bawling in another minute.

He stood and headed back to the safety of the apartment. Once there, out on the deck sunning his leg, his gun beside him, he surveyed the landscape and saw nothing out of the ordinary. He briefly studied a fisherman out on the lake in a rowboat. The man was drifting, a line in the water, while he waited for a bite. Jess recognized the man as a local.

He relaxed and continued his watch. He saw Mandy come outside and go immediately to Kate. The little girl climbed into Kate's arms and snuggled against the womanly breast, a thumb in her mouth, her manner one of total trust. A lump came into his throat and refused to be dislodged.

If he stayed, if he took a job here…

If he did, then what? Marriage and happily-ever-after with Kate and the kids? Yeah, right. He'd loved his sister but she'd left. He'd loved his mother and wife and lost them. He loved his son, but their relationship was an iffy proposition at best. Yeah, his life was just filled with happily-ever-after events. Better to return to Houston and forget such nonsense.

None of this reasoning stopped the longing, though.

He checked the lake again. The fisherman was rowing leisurely toward the ranch that adjoined the Windraven acreage. That land belonged to Kate's mother-in-law, who now lived with her daughter in another state. Kris had grown up next door to Kate, albeit several years before she did. Still, the two of them shared a legacy of the land, the mountains and the small town nestled at the end of the valley.

What did he have to offer a woman? For the first time he wanted a real answer to the question. None came to him.

"Come in, Jess, and have a seat," Shannon invited, closing a file on her computer. "What brings you to town?" She glanced at the folder in his hand.

Jess took the seat she indicated. He laid the report from the sheriff's archives on the corner of her desk. "Curiosity," he informed her. He gestured toward the file. "There are no pictures of the boat when she went down. Surely the diver made some of the wreck."

She flipped through the reports she had gathered for him. "Did you check the newspaper articles on it?"

"Yes. They had a snapshot of Herriot on the boat when he was teaching a class on sailing for the local community college. Nothing else."

"Hmm. Wait a sec and I'll check my files." She called up the list of stored evidence and quickly sorted through it. "There's a number missing in the archives on the case, like maybe someone deleted a piece of evidence. That can happen if it's discovered something doesn't apply."

Jess leaned across the desk and studied the screen of data. "Or if someone wants to get rid of evidence."

Shannon's expression cooled. "Maybe that happens in Houston, but not here. We don't do business by politics."

He didn't say anything, but suspicion must have shown in his eyes.

"We don't," she insisted.

He nodded grimly, gathered up the contents of the folder and prepared to leave.

"I'll check the records again," she said when he reached the door.

He turned back. Their eyes met in mutual understanding. "Thanks, Shannon. I owe you for this."

Her grin was mocking, but her eyes were serious. "I'll call you on that, one of these days."

Out in the pickup he mulled over the facts and the missing bit of data. Frowning in frustration, he drove out to the ranch, passing the road to Kate's place and going on to the main house.

Jeremy and Megan were in the arena, putting a couple of horses through their paces. He parked and walked to the fence to watch. Jeremy's mount balked at the jump.

"Give him a tap with the switch," Megan called.

The youngster brought the big gelding around to the jump again, then whisked a short riding crop across the horse's hindquarters just as they approached the jump. Startled, the horse leaped sideways instead of heading over the low white pole raised between two other poles. Jeremy made the jump on his own, sailing out of the saddle and over the pole in a graceful arc before landing on his front with an audible "whoof" as the breath was knocked out of him. He lay in the dust without moving.

Jess reacted before he thought. He dropped the cane and climbed over the fence. He was conscious of a flare of pain when he dropped to the ground, but it was quickly forgotten as he knelt beside his son.

"Hey," he said as calmly as he could, "you okay?" He ran his hands over the boy's arms and legs.

"Yes," Jeremy mouthed, rolling over and up to a sitting position. He opened his mouth and tried to suck in a breath. Startled, he stared at Jess, panic in his eyes.

"It'll be okay," Jess said in calming tones. "You got the breath knocked out of you. I'll help you out."

He pushed the boy supine on the ground and used part of his CPR training to gently force breath back into the boy's lungs. On the third try, he felt his son's diaphragm expand on its own. Jeremy pulled in air in shallow gasps.

"Never…had that…happen before," he said, sitting up again.

"It's scary, but your body recovers sooner or later on its own. It's easier if it has a kick start."

"You had it happen…to you?" Jeremy asked, breathing deeper now.

"A couple of times." Jess grinned at his son, feeling the camaraderie of shared experience.

After a second Jeremy grinned back.

"You okay?" Megan asked, kneeling beside the two males.

Jess glanced around and saw the horses tied to the rail on the far side of the ring.

"Sure," Jeremy averred.

"Good. Can you get back on?" she asked. It was a throwaway question, as if it didn't matter one way or the other.

Jess started to protest, but held the words in. His niece was the riding expert. He'd let her call the shots.

"Uh, yeah."

Pride rushed over him. The boy was a trouper. However, his worry must have gotten through to Megan.

"I wouldn't let Jeremy get on if I thought it was unsafe. The gelding knows he did wrong. Now he has to be shown how to do right. I think he's ready."

Jeremy stood, his thin face determined. "Let's go."

"This time I want you to walk him around the ring while I jump the mare. Horses want to do what other horses are doing. Hold him in for at least three rounds, then set him at the jump after the mare has gone over and is clear.''

''Right.''

Jess walked back to the railing and climbed over. His knee was burning, but it wasn't too bad. He gritted his teeth and watched while Jeremy rode his mount around the ring, then took the jump as easily as water running downhill.

When Jeremy beamed a proud smile his way, Jess grinned and waved and, leaning on the cane, limped to the pickup. He made it to Kate's with an effort. When she saw him struggle to stand upright as he climbed out of the truck, she came running.

''What happened?'' she asked, looping an arm around him.

''Took a wrong step,'' he explained.

He let her carry part of his weight and help him to the swing on her front porch. She rolled up his pants leg, clucked over the fast-swelling knee and dashed inside. She was back in a moment with ice cubes wrapped in a dish towel. He didn't protest when she wrapped it firmly round his knee.

''Now tell me what really happened,'' she demanded after she propped a stool under his foot.

''Jeremy took a fall from a horse. I jumped into the ring.'' He gave a bitter snort of laughter. ''Buzz Lightyear to the rescue,'' he mocked himself.

''Don't,'' she chided gently. She stroked his cheek. ''It's your nature to rescue those in danger.''

''Yeah, an old war horse who can't get it through his head that he's been put out to pasture.''

''Feeling sorry for yourself, Detective?'' she said.

''Can't think what to do with your life for the next forty to fifty years? That's tough.''

''Look who's talking,'' he snapped, surprised by her tone and lack of sympathy. ''The reclusive widow, who hides herself from life by avoiding contact with anyone who might possibly stir her to feeling something real and important.''

''Sex is hardly world shaking.''

Fury overcame his sense of fair play. ''It can be. Between the right people, it can be the world.''

He realized the impact of his words a split second after uttering them. Ignoring her shocked face and the questions that raced through her expressive eyes, he flung himself off the swing with a curse and headed for the apartment, his injury be damned. His knee got him upstairs and to the sofa before collapsing on him.

Chapter Eleven

Kate conducted a futile argument with herself for the rest of the afternoon and early evening. She wanted to check on Jess, but stubborn pride intervened with its own arguments. On the one hand, he was in the apartment alone; on the other, being alone was his choice.

Jeremy hadn't come back from Megan's yet. He could be spending the night at the big house. An hour ago she'd heard the telephone ringing in the apartment. After several times it had stopped. She'd assumed Jess had answered.

On an impulse she called the ranch house and got the answering machine. Megan was still out with the horses.

Irritated, Kate went to the window and gazed up at the apartment. The windows were dark except for an eerie glow in the living room. The television was on. Her mother had always said it was bad for the eyes to watch television in an otherwise dark room.

Sighing in exasperation at her worries, she went to check on Mandy. The little girl was propped on the sofa, the stuffed bunny clasped in her arms, while she watched *Sesame Street* with bright-eyed interest.

Kate's heart somersaulted. She felt a kinship with Mandy that went beyond the maternal. The child was intelligent, resilient and incredibly brave. She'd been abandoned and put into danger by those who should have protected her. It was enough to shake a person's faith in the goodness of people.

When Mandy looked her way, Kate smiled, then sat beside the little girl and watched the remainder of the show. When it ended, Kate flicked the TV off.

"Let's go see how Jess is doing," she suggested. "He hurt his sore knee again. It might need an ice bag."

After unlocking, then locking the door behind them—which felt very strange as the house had rarely been locked during her lifetime—she and Mandy headed for the garage apartment.

Kate glanced at the garden, the shrubs around the house, the walnut trees and the cottonwoods down by the creek where it ran into the lake. Was that the shadow of a man over there behind the bushes? Why hadn't she cut them back earlier in the summer? What about the gardening shed? Anyone could hide behind it. Or in it.

Chills cascaded over her at the thought of reaching inside the low building and encountering a hand that yanked her inside and— Stop it!

Taking a deep breath, she knocked softly on the screen door to the apartment. No one answered. The wooden door was open. She peered in. No signs of life other than the evening news on television.

"Shall we go in?" she asked aloud.

Mandy nodded.

Giving the child a faint but reassuring smile, Kate opened the door, half expecting Jess to yell at her for doing so.

Inside, they found him propped on the sofa cushions, sound asleep. She flicked on a lamp and noted that the towel that had served as an ice pack around his knee had long since become soggy.

He'd placed a plastic grocery bag under another towel to catch the drip. A thoughtful man. With a smile she removed the makeshift ice pack and went to the kitchen. After wringing the water out, she added ice cubes and folded the terry cloth around them. Mandy followed at her heels.

On the counter beside the sink she found a prescription bottle of painkillers. That explained the deep sleep.

"Come on, Mandy. We'll wrap Jess's knee up and leave before the grouchy ol' bear wakes and growls at us."

Mandy clamped a hand over her mouth as she giggled at Kate's description. They tiptoed into the other room. Kate replaced the ice pack, then paused as she wondered about his dinner, or lack thereof.

It wasn't her problem. She'd let him worry about that. As she turned away, his voice caught her off guard.

"What the—" He sat up and glanced around suspiciously.

Every nerve in her body jumped.

"Kate," he mumbled, dropping back to the stack of pillows under his head. "I thought you were Collins."

"No, it's just Mandy and me."

He rolled his head and glanced at Mandy, then back to her. "So I see. I must have fallen asleep…" His voice trailed off. He gazed at the television. "It's late."

"Only six," Kate told him.

He grimaced. "Those pain pills knocked me out. I won't be taking those anymore."

"Why not? You need to rest—"

"I need to be alert," he interrupted, his expression hard and determined. He glared at her. "Are you carrying?" he asked on a lower note after another glance at Mandy

Kate shook her head. "I forgot—"

"Don't forget," he growled, swinging his legs to the floor. "It could be fatal."

"I know," she said quietly. "I'll be more careful."

He wiped a hand over his face. "Sorry. I didn't mean to snap, but one of us has to stay on guard."

"It isn't your problem, Detective," she reminded him crisply, feeling reprimanded. "We have our own cops out here."

"A heck of a lot of good they'll do you and the kid when it's too late." He paused. "Where's Jeremy?"

"Still at Megan's, I think. I called but got the answering machine. Your telephone was ringing earlier."

Before he could rise, she went to the phone and clicked the button on the answering machine. Jeremy's voice reported he was eating supper with Megan and would be home later.

"You can eat with me and Mandy," Kate said, erasing the message. "We'll bring it up here."

"Forget it. I can fend for myself."

"I know, but we're following a good-neighbor policy here. Neighbors help look out for each other." She gave him a meaningful glare.

He exhaled heavily, then nodded. "Okay, but keep an eye out, hear?"

"Yes. Come on, Mandy. Let's go fix dinner for the bear."

Mandy giggled and cast Jess a shy look.

To Kate's surprise he winked at the child before turning a scowl in *her* direction.

Much more cheerful, she prepared plates of roast beef sandwiches, potatoes and gravy and slaw at her house and placed them on a tray. Putting Mandy to work collecting and folding napkins, Kate hid the handgun under a cup towel.

"Okay, let's go," she said.

Outside, she surveyed the area carefully before proceeding to the apartment. They got there safely. Inside she set the tray on the coffee table. "Dinner, my lord," she announced.

"Thank you, my good and loyal servant," he returned in the same tone.

Mandy looked solemnly from one to the other. When they smiled, she did, too. She took a seat on the floor, the bunny beside her. Kate set a plate before each of them.

"Papa Bear's, Mama Bear's and Baby Bear's," Mandy said, pointing at the plates. Jess's held the largest serving, then Kate's, then hers.

Kate brushed the fine hair of Mandy's forehead. "That's right. We'd better eat before that bothersome little Goldilocks stops by and tries to gobble our dinner all up!"

Mandy clamped a hand over her mouth and giggled with delight. Kate vowed that someday this wonderful little girl would laugh without restraint. She looked up to find Jess's eyes on her, their depths darkly mysterious, quietly assessing as he watched her with the child. A half smile lingered at the corners of his mouth like an afterthought.

Unexpected longing filled her and was followed by unwanted visions of a future that could never be. She saw herself seated beside Jess while he held an infant in his arms. Their child.

Her eyes burned as the image faded. She longed to call it back, to cling to the futile hope of a future so far removed from reality it was foolish to even imagine it.

A touch on her arm brought her back to the present. Jess brushed her elbow lightly with a finger once more, then withdrew and began eating. Feeling oddly comforted, she, too, picked up her fork and joined in the meal.

After loading up the tray, she brought Jess two tablets of ibuprofen and a glass of water. "You'll need this. It helps stop the inflammation in your injury."

"All right," he agreed after seeing what they were. "Be careful going home. Lock all your windows."

She nodded. "Come on, Mandy. It's time to go."

Later, she caught a glimpse of Jess sitting on the deck over the garage. She recalled a phrase from the Bible—"behold the watcher on the wall." A sense of safety stole over her. It remained all evening as she supervised Mandy's bath, then tucked the child into bed with a prayer and good-night kiss.

When she went to bed, Jess was still there, silhouetted by the moonlight. It was nice to have someone who cared enough to watch over them.

But, she warned, don't get used to it. She smiled, feeling tender and sad at the same time.

Kate woke with her heart pounding. She lay still, her eyes flicking over the shadows in the room. Glancing at the window, she was surprised by the gray tints of early dawn. She'd slept deeply through the night. At the moment she didn't know what had startled her out of sleep, but during her years with Kris she had learned to be careful. Some noise, one not associated with the regular sounds of the household, had disturbed her enough to bring her to instant wakefulness.

Listening intently, she identified the soft hum of the refrigerator in the kitchen. No other sound rippled the quiet of the house.

She didn't relax. Instead, she slipped out of bed and silently pulled on dark sweats after dropping her gown on a chair. She picked up the gun and was glad of its cool I-mean-business solidity against her palm.

More confident, she walked barefoot to the open

door, but didn't present a profile to be detected in the faint light from the windows. Instead she crouched against the wall, then ducked through the doorway into the darker shadows of the hall.

Nothing stirred.

The hair rose on her nape. The house was too quiet. She knew something was wrong, knew it with the gut-deep instinct of survival, just as she had during those last years of her marriage. Only she hadn't thought the danger was aimed at her at that time; now she knew it was. Ray Collins would kill anyone who got in the way.

To protect Mandy she had to stop him first. She wondered if she could shoot a man, then worried that she wouldn't be able to if the situation became critical.

Drawing on all her reserves of courage, she moved silently down the hall toward Mandy's room. When she opened the door, she somehow knew what she would see.

The bed was empty. There was no sign of the child…or an intruder.

With a muffled cry of rage and pain, Kate flicked on the light. "Mandy?" she called, hoping against logic that the child was someplace in the house.

No answer.

With a sick feeling Kate conducted a cursory search of the house. Downstairs she found the kitchen door unlocked, the window pane missing. Collins had somehow removed it and simply reached inside and let himself in.

Outside, she heard the sound of tires on gravel. She dashed into the yard. A pickup was going down the drive without its headlights on. Jess came out of the apartment.

"Jess!" she shouted. "Jess! It's Collins! He has Mandy!"

In the faint light she saw the gleam of metal in his hand, then a series of flashes and the sound of several shots as he fired at the truck. She pressed a hand to her mouth, fear of Mandy's being hit washing over her like a tidal wave.

To her astonishment, the truck veered sharply, righted itself, then went into a skid. Jess had hit a tire! The truck careened to a stop, its fender against a tree.

She broke into a run, one thought on her mind— get Mandy away from Collins.

"Kate, stay back!" Jess yelled at her.

She ignored him until she saw a flash out of the dark at the edge of the woods and heard the retort. Collins was firing at them. In the silence after the shots, she heard Mandy scream in terror.

"Let her go!" she demanded, running forward once more. "She's only a child. Let her go or... or—"

A hand caught her arm and yanked her around. "Don't be a fool," Jess ordered roughly. "You can't catch him alone. Call the sheriff."

"He'll get away," she protested.

"I'll track him. Get going. The faster we throw up a dragnet, the faster we'll get Mandy back."

Nodding, she ran to the house and dialed 911 on the kitchen phone. She quickly informed the dispatcher what had happened. A moment later the sheriff came on the line.

"Is he alone?" Gene asked.

"He's got Mandy."

"No other adults with him?"

"No. Please, please hurry."

"I'm in my cruiser and on the way," he assured her. "The state police and FBI will work with us. We'll meet at your place. Stay there. I'll need someone to give us Collins's direction."

"He's in the woods between my house and the lake. He's armed. He fired at us after Jess shot his back tire out."

"Good man," the sheriff approved. "Collins will be easier to catch on foot."

The sheriff sounded almost jovial at this turn of events. Kate hung up, not the least reassured. A person could easily hide in the thousands of acres of wilderness surrounding the lake without being detected. There had been that case in another state where a man had evaded the FBI for months. Here, there were caves and ravines and boulder fields big enough to hide a tank.

Taking the portable phone with her, she went outside. Jess was just heading out, Jeremy with him. She crossed the lawn and reported the sheriff was on the way.

"Did he say he was bringing dogs?" Jess asked.

"No. I didn't think to ask. I'll call—"

"He'll think of it," Jess interrupted. "Meanwhile I'll keep the pressure on Collins. He can't hole up with someone close on his trail."

"Maybe you should wait for the police," she said, walking with them to the woods where the convict had disappeared. "He may hide and wait for you."

"I doubt it, not with a kid to keep quiet, too." He cast her an odd look, one that was almost tender. He glanced at his son. "You stay with Kate. See that she doesn't do anything foolish."

"I want to go with you," Jeremy protested.

"Not this time."

Although his chin set in an obstinate manner, Jeremy didn't argue with the stern order.

Kate continued to worry. Collins was armed and desperate and, in her opinion, insane. He wouldn't give up easily if Jess came upon him.

She watched Jess check the ground and wondered how fast and how far he could go with his injury. His limp was pronounced even though he was using the cane.

Clutching the gun that had proven useless as a barrier to the kidnapping, she retreated to the house. Jeremy plopped on the front porch steps and watched his dad disappear. She sympathized with the boy. Waiting was hard.

Checking the back door, she found Collins had simply pried off the wood trim, then laid it and the glass pane on a wicker table. She nailed the window back in place.

After putting a chair under the doorknob of the back door in addition to locking it, she went out and sat on the front steps. Jeremy was nowhere in sight.

Before she could check the apartment, the sheriff drove up. Five other patrol cars arrived on his heels. One patrolman had a pack of dogs in the back of his SUV.

"I've called in the state police," Gene told her.

"We're going to circle the lake. I'd like to catch Collins before he gets into the forest on the other side."

"Jess is tracking him. He said he'd leave a trail for you to follow."

Gene nodded. "Damn good man," he muttered before turning away to issue orders to his men and consult with the state patrolman who had arrived on the scene.

Kate looked at the peaks rising from the mist on the far side of the lake. There were dangerous ridges with steep drop-offs on either side along the mountain trails. If Mandy struggled, she could cause her father to fall. If she broke away and ran, she could go right over a cliff before she saw it in time to stop. There were mountain lions and bears, coyotes and bobcats. A little girl would be easy prey.

She pressed her lips together to stop the wail of despair that filled her throat. The moment when she'd lost her unborn son rolled over her, only now the terror was for Mandy. *Please, please,* she silently prayed.

When the sheriff dispersed his men, Kate looked for Jeremy. She didn't find the boy anywhere. Glancing toward the woods where Jess had disappeared, she knew the son had followed his father. She reported this information to the sheriff.

"We'll keep an eye out for him," Gene promised.

An hour later, with no results, Kate dialed Megan's house. The two cousins knew the mountains better than any of the sheriff's deputies. If Collins made it to the National Forest land, he would probably stay on a trail to make better time. Snow shelters dotted the forest, primitive log cabins built for hikers to wait out a storm. There were abandoned mining sites with crude huts. Collins could take refuge in any of those.

Thanks to Kris and his dementia, she knew where all of them were. She also knew how to survive in the wilderness. Did Collins? An icy calm settled inside her.

When Megan answered the phone, Kate told her what had happened. "Bring horses. We'll go up into the hills if the dragnet fails."

"Right," Megan said. "Riding will be faster."

By noon, Kate knew the escaped convict had eluded the sheriff and his men. Jess and Jeremy had also disappeared. The sheriff was furious that some of the men had gone beyond the boundaries he'd set and wiped out any trail they had left.

Megan stayed close to Kate, both women silent as the search perimeters were enlarged again, then again. Shannon, on duty in town, called to reassure them.

At midafternoon, Kate nudged Megan. "Let's go."

The base of operations had moved to the lakeside. No one was there to see them collect the horses from the shade beside the garage. No one was there to stop them as they trotted up the road and entered the woods on a little-used trail that would take them miles into the forest and up toward the icy peaks.

Jess almost fell onto a boulder. His knee had buckled more than once in the last hour. It burned steadily now and he could no longer ignore it.

"He's doubled back or something," Jeremy decided, sitting on another boulder and wiping sweat from his face with the hem of his T-shirt.

Jess, picking up sound behind him, had found his

son on the trail an hour after starting. Knowing he wasn't going to catch up to Collins, and not wanting to lose time taking the boy back, he'd let Jeremy tag along—after a brief but furious lecture on following orders and the promise of a hiding in the future if he disobeyed again.

He looked at the rocky talus across the slope in front of them. "Unless he went across that."

Jeremy looked doubtful. "It's awfully dangerous, especially with a little kid."

"A desperate man takes chances."

They looked beyond the rock field to the forest that angled sharply upward. The trees thinned out a thousand feet above them, then disappeared as the land changed to rugged alpine peaks and tundra. A waterfall, fine as a silk veil, dropped two hundred feet into a granite pool above the tree line. The sky was a brilliant azure. The sunlight dazzled the eye as it bounced off snow lying in a glacial cirque.

The scene was one of breathtaking beauty, and Jess thought of Kate. He'd like to share it with her.

He pushed the thought away as soon as it appeared. It would be a far stretch for him to walk up here again, if ever.

"Dad?" Jeremy questioned, uncertainty in the word.

"I can't make it any farther," Jess admitted. "The knee won't hold out."

Jeremy was silent for a moment. "I'll see if I can pick up the trail on the other side of the rocks. That way, when the sheriff gets here, we can tell him if the trail continues up the mountain or down."

Before Jess could refuse, the boy loped off, his long legs measuring out the ground in sure-footed swaths.

"Don't go out of hearing," he called as Jeremy slowed and carefully picked a path across the loose, rocky debris of the slope. Jess felt a moment of pride as well as envy.

Washed up.

The past eight hours had proved that fact conclusively. He wasn't sure he could get back down the mountain. He knew he couldn't go on up even if Jeremy did pick up the trail.

The sense of failure settled like a black cloak around him. Kate loved the little girl. He'd wanted to be the one to bring the kid back to her, to see the relief and joy in her eyes, to experience her gratitude—

Hell, what was he thinking like that for? Capturing madmen was for heroes, not a crippled ex-cop who couldn't climb a damn hill.

He frowned at the trees beyond the rocks. Where was Jeremy? The boy had made it across and gone into the forest on the other side. It was time to start back if they were going to make it before dark.

"Jer?" he called.

No one answered. An eerie feeling crept down his spine. He stood, leaning heavily on his cane. His son had gone on, climbing toward danger. The sense of it filled the air all around him. He called twice more and got no answer.

Kate's heart jumped to her throat when she saw a lone figure standing on the trail ahead of them.

"You need a lift, stranger?" she asked, riding up

to Jess. He tossed a hard glance her way, then stared at the rockslide along the mountain's flank.

"No," he said.

"Did you see Collins come this way?" Megan demanded.

"I followed his trail until we hit this ridge. It's too rocky to leave prints, or else he's trickier than we thought," Jess told them. "Jeremy went across the slope to see if he could pick up a sign. He's been gone over twenty minutes."

Kate's eyes met Megan's as she picked up on the father's concern. Both added the boy's safety to their other worries. She turned back to Jess. "This trail winds around and joins the other one farther up the mountain. If Jeremy's following the bluff trail, we'll pick it up a half mile from here. We can backtrack and find him."

"I'll go," Jess said, rising. "Give me your horse. You two can get back to the house before dark—"

"No way. Megan and I aren't leaving." Kate returned Jess's glare without flinching. When he sighed, she knew she'd won. Kicking her foot free of the stirrup and sliding forward, she told him, "Climb on. We'll make better time on horseback than you can on foot."

"Right," he agreed sarcastically. "As if I could walk."

"I wasn't going to mention your being a cripple and all," she told him right back without a trace of the sympathy she actually felt.

Megan's eyebrows rose at this jab, but she said nothing while Jess mounted behind Kate. When he was ready, Kate clicked to the gelding, and they continued along the trail that appeared to go in the opposite direction from where they wanted.

After a few yards they came to a hairpin curve. Five more turns brought them out on a ridge above the talus slope and to the fork that led back to where Jeremy had crossed the boulders and started up.

"Timber Wolf," Megan suggested.

Kate nodded. "Or Snowy Ridge."

"What are you two talking about?" Jess demanded.

"Places where Collins might have gone," Kate explained. "Both those have cabins where he could hole up."

"There're mining shafts, too," Megan reminded her. "Some deep enough to shelter a person from the weather."

Kate frowned as she stared up the winding trail. "Another tenth of a mile and we'll be out of the trees."

"Is there rock cover?" Jess asked.

"Some." She glanced over her shoulder, aware of his heat at her back. "It'll be cold up here tonight. Mandy doesn't have a coat, only the T-shirt she sleeps in. He didn't take any clothes for her, other than her sneakers."

Jess's hands tightened at her waist. "We'll find her. We'll get her back to you."

"Not tonight," Megan said. "We can't reach the first cabin before dark. It's dangerous to travel after that. We'll have to go back."

"Do we?" Jess asked, leaving the decision to Kate.

"Yes," she said. "Megan's right. It's too dangerous. We'll go down this way and pick Jeremy up."

They turned onto the downward trail.

"We'll come back at first light," Jess promised in a low husky tone as they rode down.

His arms circled and held her in a gentle embrace while worry ate at her. "I hope he doesn't frighten her," she said.

"She's brave, Katie. Like you."

Kate shook her head. "I persevere, but I'm not brave."

His breath stroked her temple and his hands tightened as the gelding stumbled, then caught itself on the dangerous trail. "You don't know yourself," he told her.

They didn't meet Jeremy along the trail. Jess climbed down and searched for footprints. After ten minutes he found a couple. "He was going up," he said, straightening. "I told him not to go out of hearing."

"He's stubborn like his father," Megan said. "Let's start from here in the morning. There's nothing we can do at night."

Kate ached for Jess on the way down. While he didn't say anything, his concern over his son was palpable. After dropping them at the house, Megan rode off, leading the gelding.

"Come on. We have to have something to eat." Kate led the way into the house. She turned on lights and checked for messages. Gene had left one on her machine.

"We'll be at the lake. I've moved operations over to the Herriot ranch. We'll start from there in the morning. You stay put at your place, you hear?"

The machine clicked off. She looked at Jess.

"Nothing is ever as simple as it should be. Capture an escaped convict on foot? Should be a snap with the county and state police after him, not to mention the FBI, which will be brought in."

She pressed a hand against her mouth to stop the trembling of her lips. Jess took two steps forward. His arms slid around her. "We'll get our kids back."

"Don't promise what you can't deliver." She tried to sound cynical, but all that came out was despair.

He grimaced. Letting her go, he limped to a chair and sat heavily. "How about that dinner you mentioned earlier?"

Kate was aware of his eyes following her as she moved about the kitchen. The ritual of meal preparation helped restore her composure, although she didn't feel any more hopeful. The emptiness beat at her. For the past few days it had receded, but now it was back, and she was afraid. The night was cold; the children were so vulnerable.

By the time they sat down to eat, the sky had grown dark. Across the lake she could see lights in the Herriot boathouse and along the pier. The bloodhounds howled as they were penned for the night. In the mountains a lone coyote joined in, then another and another. The long moaning howls continued until they circled the mountains like an evil omen.

"Wolves?" Jess asked, his eyes dark with worry.

"Not likely. We haven't had wolves in these parts in a hundred years." She didn't mention the mountain lions and bears that were more dangerous to a lone boy than a pack of wolves or coyotes. Canines couldn't climb trees.

After eating, they sat on the swing in the dark and stared at the peaks surrounding the valley.

Jess rose. "I'd better head in. As someone once said—tomorrow is another day."

"Stay," she murmured, laying her hand on his arm.

"Stay?"

"Yes. With me. I need you."

He let out a harsh breath, then drew her to her feet. "This might be a mistake," he warned.

"I don't care." At the moment, she didn't. "I need your warmth, your strength…" Her voice choked and died away on the chilly night wind.

They went inside, not bothering to lock the door. That had already proven futile in stopping an intruder. Upstairs they paused beside the bed and slowly undressed.

"Take what you need," he murmured, holding her close. "I'll give all I can."

She clung to him as the night shut them in and blocked the mountains from view. Along the river the ravens cawed.

"The ravens," she said.

"Don't listen."

He tucked her into bed and touched her until finally all she could hear was the sound of her heart and his, beating together in despair and desperate passion.

Chapter Twelve

Jess woke, fully alert, to the sound of the phone. It was answered on the first ring. He grabbed the bed-side extension. When he heard Megan's voice, he hung up quietly. He'd been tensed for bad news, he realized.

Checking the sky through the lace curtains, he saw the sun wasn't up. The clock indicated it wasn't quite five.

He stretched, feeling more rested than he had in months. After the fierce lovemaking, Kate had insisted on going to his house and getting two of the painkillers the doctor had prescribed. He'd taken them, but not until after she'd pointed out he wouldn't be of any use on the search in his present condition. That had struck home.

After that he'd sunk into a deep, dreamless sleep

occasionally broken by her restless cries as nightmares haunted her sleep. He wondered if she'd slept any.

Worry eating at him, he showered and dressed in the clean clothes she'd also brought back from his place. After checking his gun and the extra clips, he headed downstairs.

The house seemed strangely empty, almost bereft, without Mandy's or Jeremy's lively presence. Kids. They changed a person's perspective. He pressed a hand to the quick ache in his chest.

He found Kate in the kitchen, packing lunches. She smiled—quickly, worriedly, but a smile—when he appeared. "Good, you're up. Megan just called. She's on her way with mounts for us. I'm packing lunches for everyone. For Mandy and Jeremy, too."

Abruptly she turned back to the sink, her head lowered as she sought for control. Jess went to her. Laying his hands on her shoulders, he held her close, knowing words wouldn't erase or ease her despair. He was surprised at how much he longed to comfort her.

"I'm so afraid for them," she whispered.

"I know. We'll do all we can. Our best, Kate. So will the sheriff."

"I have breakfast ready," she said, brave and composed once more. "We'd better eat."

Jess poured a cup of coffee while she set bacon and eggs and toast on the table. They ate without talking. The sun was just peeking above the horizon when they finished, and Megan rode up. Kate went to the door and asked if Megan had eaten.

"Yes," the cousin called. "Are you ready to go?"

"Be with you in a minute."

The cold air circulated through the warm kitchen from the open door. Jess thought of the night and the warmth of Kate's bed, then of Mandy and Jeremy someplace on the mountain without jackets. Pain grabbed at him and wouldn't let go.

"Ready?" Kate asked him. She stowed dishes in the dishwasher, her movements hurried and jerky.

"Yes."

"Let's go."

Jess carried the bag of sandwiches, fruit and cookies outside. Megan indicated they could go in a saddlebag on the gelding Kate had ridden the previous day. He noted she had a shotgun in a scabbard attached to her saddle.

"The gelding is yours," she said. "Kate can ride the mare."

He nodded and swung up, not without a grunt of effort as his left leg took his weight. Kate put her foot in the stirrup and leaped on the mare's back in one motion.

"Did you bring coats for Jeremy and Mandy?" Megan asked, eyeing the bundle Kate had tied behind her saddle.

"Yes."

"Then let's be off." Megan led the way.

"You got your gun?" Jess asked, following the women.

Kate nodded.

He wished he could make everything right for her and, for a second, experienced the futility of their efforts. Love. Attachments. Caring. They made a person hurt in ways bullets never could.

Riding single file up the trail, they veered to the right before reaching the rock slide and joining the other trail they had followed yesterday up above the fault. A little ways up, he spotted a tree limb bent at a downward angle, then two more.

"Jeremy's been through here," he told the other two. "He's marked the path."

"The question is, did Collins also go this way?" Megan speculated aloud. "There are so many places he could hide—"

She broke off with an apologetic glance over her shoulder at Kate. Jess gave her a look that willed her to stop talking and ride. She got the message. For the next two hours she urged her mount to pick up the pace at every opportunity.

He was beginning to feel the hardness of saddle leather when she stopped beside a tiny mountain creek. "The horses need to rest," she announced.

Kate slipped out of the saddle and led her horse to a spot beside the creek. The mare drank her fill, her ears flicking first one way, then another. Megan's horses did the same.

Jess dismounted, managed to keep the groan silent and let the gelding pick its own drinking spot. Observing the rugged terrain, he admitted he could never have made it this far without the horse. His knee was beginning to ache steadily now.

It occurred to him that a man didn't have to be superhuman, that there were other ways to accomplish the same goals. Kate and her cousin had known that from the first.

He sat on a boulder and took three ibuprofen tablets with a slug of water, also packed by Kate. When he looked up, he found her eyes on him. He smiled to ease her worry.

She came over and sat near him. "Are you in pain?"

"It's not bad. I'll be okay."

"This vacation hasn't been very restful for you." Her slight smile indicated irony.

"I'll make up for it when Collins is behind bars again."

She stared up the trail. "What if we don't find him?"

"Jeremy left us a trail. He would have come back yesterday if he hadn't been sure he was tracking Collins."

"He's brave. Like his father," she added softly. "I'm glad you came to the ranch, both of you."

"Even if it hurts when we leave?"

She hesitated, then nodded. "Even then."

Her gaze was level and unflinching. She was brave, this woman. She could face anything. Admiration and other emotions whirled through the confines of his soul. He wished he could give her rainbows and all the good things in life.

Megan ran her hands over the legs of each horse. "Okay, we can go on up."

"Wait here," Kate told him.

She brought the gelding over to the boulder. By standing on it, he found he could mount much easier. "Thanks."

She gave him a sympathetic glance and brought the mare over so she could also mount from the boulder. "It's been a while since I've done any serious riding," she explained when Megan looked a question her way.

Kate kept an eye on Jess as the trail grew steeper, not that she thought he would have trouble staying on, but that he might be in pain and refuse to admit it. After he'd gone to sleep, she'd placed a bag of ice on either side of his knee. Later she'd refilled them, then later still, she'd done it again. She'd removed them and gotten up for the last time when the sky began to brighten.

Megan held up her hand, and the little cavalcade stopped. Kate nodded when her cousin glanced at her.

"We're close to the first snow shelter," she said in a near whisper to Jess. "We should walk from here and check it out before going in."

The three of them dismounted and led the horses for another few yards. Then they tied the reins to shrubs and left the horses munching at the sparse vegetation beneath the thinning trees.

Jess took the lead. "How far to the cabin?" he asked.

"Just around that next bend and to the right. It's hard to see in the trees surrounding it," Megan explained softly.

"The trees will give us cover," he said. "Keep them between you and the cabin."

Kate nodded along with Megan. Jess bent and studied the trail, then, seemingly satisfied, walked on. The women followed. Megan tapped him on the shoulder and pointed through the patch of pines at the one-room hut off to the side after they had gone several yards along the trail. He nodded and picked a circular path toward the place.

After several minutes of watching without seeing any signs of activity, he motioned for them to stay put while he crept up to the back of the cabin. Kate checked her weapon and prepared to cover the front in case Collins came running out.

The back of her neck prickled as the silence lengthened. A bird flew up under the eaves of the tiny cabin and disappeared.

"No one's there," Megan said.

Kate nodded. "The bird wouldn't have gone in if people were inside. Unless they were all asleep."

Or dead.

Her breath caught. She dismissed the thought with an angry shake of the head. No one was dead. A shot fired up here would have been heard all the way across the valley. Megan walked along the faint trail toward the shelter.

"It's okay," Jess called. "It's empty."

Kate fetched the horses and brought them with her into the clearing directly in front of the cabin.

"No one's stopped here as far as I can tell," he told them when Kate joined him and Megan.

Kate didn't voice the worry they all felt. What if Collins had Jeremy as well as Mandy? The youth would mean nothing to the convict. With a heavy heart, she rode on up the trail behind Megan. The ravens, she recalled, had been restless last night.

Jess took his place behind her. She realized he rode there to protect her back. Twisting in the saddle, she looked at him. His eyes were on the landscape around them. They flicked past her, then returned.

For a minute they observed each other, then he went back to perusing the land, his expression bleak.

Facing front, she felt the loneliness of being closed out. He had withdrawn from any emotional involvement between them.

The crisis with the kidnapping and the disappearance of his son made him too vulnerable. She knew the feeling. They had turned to each other last night out of desperation. With the dawn, he had retreated. She hadn't expected more.

In the distance she heard the harsh cry of a blue jay. It reverberated through the vast forest. Glancing at the sky, she saw clouds gathering over Medicine Bow peak. She hadn't thought to pack rain ponchos. Silently she prayed for the rain to hold off, for Collins to come to his senses, for the children to be safe, for life, just once, to be fair.

Kate drank deeply from the water bottle, pushed the spout closed and stuck the bottle back in her pack. It was almost noon, and the day had warmed considerably. She'd removed her jacket hours ago. So had Megan and Jess.

Glancing at them, she saw everything she was feeling in their set faces—anger, worry, determination, an unwillingness to admit they might fail, the fear that they would.

They couldn't fail, not this time, she protested. She couldn't go through that again. To lose Mandy just as she'd come to know and love the brave little girl… It was unthinkable.

Megan stopped at a fork in the trail. She twisted around in the saddle. ''Up to Snowy Ridge or down to the old logging site?'' she asked.

Jess climbed off the gelding with a low grunt of

pain when his left leg touched the ground. He studied the area, then pointed to an arrow marked on the ground as if someone had dragged a toe along the dust.

"This way," he said, pointing at the trail that led back down the mountain and into the thick stand of trees in the National Forest.

"Are you sure?" Megan asked. "There's nowhere close to stay—"

"The old logging trailer was left on the site when the company finished that section," Kate broke in. She leaned over the mare's neck and studied the sign. "Jess is right. Jeremy left us a clue. Let's go," she said impatiently. They were closing in on Collins. She could feel it. The mare pranced and circled as if catching her excitement.

"Easy," Jess said.

Meeting his eyes, they shared a moment of understanding. She knew they were vulnerable at the present, sharing worry over the children, combining their efforts in the search, bringing the heartaches of a past they couldn't change and a future they couldn't foresee along on the search. It created bonds that reached right down to that place of lost dreams, a place neither of them had wanted disturbed.

However, that wasn't possible. To love, whether a child or another adult, was to open yourself to hope. With hope came dreams of a future. She kept seeing them as a family.

"It will be all right," she said, needing to believe it.

He gave her a look of pity, gentleness, regret and other emotions too complex to read, then remounted.

They rode on in silence. Thirty minutes later they found Jeremy.

"Dear God," Kate said on a gasp, taking in the situation at a glance.

Jeremy rubbed his arms as chills attacked him and wished the trees didn't shade out the sun. The forest had thickened as the land dropped down a few hundred feet, then suddenly disappeared. He'd come to a ridge overlooking a clear-cut logging area.

The logging road, rough and already covered with pines and cedars about a foot tall, led downward. From this vantage point he noted the cut made by the road along several ridges that dropped in a series all the way down the mountain.

His heart lightened as he realized he could take the paved road in the distance back to Kate's place, which would be easier than the trail he'd climbed.

Guilt flashed through him for disobeying his father. He hadn't meant to keep going, but he'd found the imprint of a sneaker and had been sure it was Mandy's, so he'd followed along, going farther and farther. Until it was dark and too late to turn back. Stupid, really stupid.

He'd spent the night at the base of a tree, leaves and pine boughs for a blanket. His dad would probably ground him for life when he caught up. Even so, Jeremy hoped his father and Kate found the signs he'd left.

A few minutes later he spotted the gleam of sunlight off metal. He slid behind a thick incense cedar and peered at an old trailer sitting in a clear spot.

Hardly daring to breathe, he tried to recall what his dad had said about confronting criminals, especially one with a hostage and a gun.

Moving off the faint path, he headed up, slipping from tree to tree and staying in the deepest shadows. He paused now and again to study the trailer. No signs of life, but maybe Mandy and her father were asleep. Or dead. Or maybe they'd been here, but had left at first light. He liked that idea better.

Choosing a circular route up the mountain, he crept closer. He would see if anyone was inside. If so, he'd sit tight and wait for backup. That's what a good cop did, his dad had told him. Scout the area, make a plan, wait for reinforcements.

Bending low, he crept behind a willow thicket surrounding a pine tree. He was close to the trailer. After a minute he risked a quick peek inside and looked directly at the back of a man's head.

The escaped convict wore a baseball cap, a long-sleeved shirt and jeans. He was seated at a rickety table. Mandy was sitting on the other side, wearing a man's shirt buttoned around her. On the grimy table sat a bottle of liquor. Collins lifted it toward his mouth. As he did, Jeremy caught a glimpse of the gun that was also on the table.

Ducking down, he tried to think, to decide what his dad would do. From a distance a bird trilled a question. From farther away, another answered. Then the woods were silent. Fear lodged in his throat and blurred his eyes as he realized how *alone* he was. Blinking hard, he wished his father would hurry and show up.

* * *

"Stay here," Jess ordered the two women. "I'll go down."

"Collins must be inside," Kate said, voicing the thought that had sprung to mind when they saw Jeremy look in the trailer, then duck out of sight like a startled deer.

Jess dismounted and tied the gelding to a sapling. "Yeah. Call the sheriff and tell him where we are. Keep your guns handy and stay out of sight. Try not to interfere. There's enough to worry about without you two charging in."

He gave them a stern look to let them know he meant business, before checking his gun and the extra clips.

"All right," Kate agreed. She pulled the mobile phone from her pocket, dialed a number and put it to her ear.

Her eyes, when she glanced at him, were eerily calm, as if she'd removed herself from all feelings. He paused, but there were no words of assurance he could truly offer, and he wouldn't mouth the usual platitudes, not to Kate.

Leaving them, he stayed in the shadows and moved as quickly as he could to the place where he'd last seen Jeremy. As he came close, he had to slow down and watch out for twigs that would snap and give away his presence. Finally he spotted his son behind a willow thicket. Jeremy was peering in the back window of an old trailer, his finger over his lips.

What the hell did he think he was doing?

Ignoring the fear, Jess moved behind the willows, then murmured his son's name in a barely audible whisper.

Jeremy whipped around, his eyes wide and frightened. Relief spread into a huge grin. Jess hooked a hand around his son's neck and hauled him into his arms. Scoldings could come later. Right now he needed contact. Jeremy hugged him back as hard as he could. Jess smiled grimly and tilted his head toward the trailer.

"Mandy and her dad," Jeremy mouthed. "He's drinking. And he has a gun."

Jess nodded. Striving for the professional distance he needed, he looked inside the trailer. Mandy saw him. Her eyes widened and a grin split her face. He put a finger to his lips and shook his head in quick jerks. She didn't make a sound.

He felt Jeremy tense when they heard Collins ask in a snarly voice. "What are you grinning about?"

"Nothing," the child replied quickly.

"Life ain't nothing to laugh about," Collins continued as if his daughter hadn't spoken. "Ain't worth the worry."

"Can we go home, Daddy?"

"Don't have no home, kid. Don't have nothing."

There was a long pause followed by the sound of glass clinking. Another drink of booze, Jess surmised.

"Kate has a home. She said I could live there with her. Kate said she would adopt-shun me."

"No kid of mine is gonna be adopted by one of them do-gooders. Always looking down on a person, acting like they got the secrets of life locked inside them. Know everything, they do. Always telling a man where he's wrong. Just like my old lady. Well, look where she is today. Nowhere."

A drunken laugh followed this tirade. Jess risked

another peek. The door was opposite the window. There appeared to be only one. He needed to get the girl away from the father. The man was talking himself into a rage.

Collins picked up the gun and studied it for a long minute. "It's time," he said cryptically. "We're getting out of here before some of your friends show up. I'll shoot them if they do. Don't think I won't."

The man's tone changed to threatening. He wasn't suicidal...yet. Jess relaxed somewhat while considering a plan.

"But we'll be gone before they get here," Collins finished in a crafty voice. "Long gone." He laughed again as if at a big joke only he knew. "Put your shoes on. Hurry up."

Jess decided on a strategy. He raised up so Mandy could see him and mouthed a word, then gestured toward the tree.

"I need to go potty," Mandy told her father.

Collins lurched to his feet and reached for the door. "Well, hurry it up then," he said. He stepped outside.

Jess bent down. "When Mandy comes out, I want you to take her to the top of the ridge. Kate and Megan are there," he whispered in Jeremy's ear. "Can you do that?"

Jeremy nodded, his face unusually pale. He was taking the situation seriously and would follow orders.

With an urgency caused by intuitive knowledge that the father was near the breaking point, Jess sprinted toward one end of the trailer. Collins stared at the peaks around them then disappeared around the far corner. Jess dashed inside the open door. "Come on," he said to Mandy. "Let's go."

She finished tying her shoe and hopped out of the chair. "Where's Kate?" she asked, raising her arms to be lifted.

"Coming. I want you to go with Jeremy," he said, and headed out the door and up the slope toward the woods.

"Hey," a rough voice yelled behind them.

Jeremy stuck his head up. "Go," Jess said, pushing Mandy toward the boy, then turning to guard their flight.

Jeremy didn't need a second command. Grabbing her hand, he and Mandy ran as fast as they could for the logging trail.

Jess realized Jeremy was heading for the ridge where the trail started down instead of the one at the top of the clearing. They were in the open now, easy targets.

Collins appeared at the end of the trailer, pistol in hand. A shot rang out, reverberating off the peaks like thunder. The kids kept running.

Fury boiled through Jess. "Collins," he yelled. "Over here."

The man swung around as Jess had intended and pointed the gun at him. Jeremy, after one terrified glance back continued his dash for the road, Mandy struggling to keep up.

"Police," Jess called, moving forward. "Drop the gun. Put your hands behind your head."

Instead of obeying, Collins fired another shot, this time at Jess. He dived and rolled. When he came to his feet, Collins was nowhere in sight. Jess bent low and glanced all around.

"He's after the children!" Kate called from the ridge above them. "At the bluff above the logging road!" She pointed frantically.

Jess forgot about cover. He forgot about his knee. Time slowed as he ran as hard as he could toward the bluff where the road made a hairpin turn around the slope. Collins stood on the rocky ledge. He aimed the pistol at a sharp downward angle, vile words spewing from his mouth as he vented his rage.

Jess lifted the 9 mm semiautomatic. Collins might fire when he was hit, but it was a chance the detective had to take. He tried not to think of his son or the child or Kate's grief if he failed. He squeezed the trigger.

He saw Collins's arm jerk from the recoil as the convict shot off a round, then he seemed to jerk all over. He spun about as if in surprise, teetered on the ledge, then fell in a slow, graceful arc, disappearing from sight.

"Thank God," Megan said behind Jess, her voice angry and unforgiving. "I hope he's gone."

"Me, too," he agreed.

Kate rode close to the cliff and dismounted, her face pale. Jess came over, his limp pronounced, but he couldn't help that at the moment. Collins lay on the rocks a few feet below.

"The sheriff can pick him up later," Jess said, feeling so utterly weary he could hardly stand. The letdown following an adrenaline high. He knew the signs.

"Where are the children?" Kate asked.

"Jeremy," Jess called out near the edge.

"Here," Jeremy answered. He crawled out from behind a stump. Mandy was behind him.

"Stay there," Jess told them. "We'll be right down."

He picked his way down the rocky bluff while Kate and Megan brought the horses around the road.

"Dad, I'm sorry," Jeremy said as soon as Jess drew close. The boy's face was so white every freckle stood out. "I went the wrong way."

Jess just shook his head, then hauled his son into his arms. "You did good," he said. "You did really good. Collins is…" He looked at Mandy, then at Jeremy. "He's gone."

"He shot at us," Jeremy said in a disbelieving voice. "He meant…he meant to…"

"I know."

The little girl stood so still and quiet she might have been invisible. Anger boiled anew in Jess. No child should ever have to be that scared. He enclosed her, very gently, in his embrace, too. She trembled violently in every muscle.

"It's okay, honey," he whispered. "It's okay."

Chapter Thirteen

Kate leaped from her mount, when she and Megan finally got down the slope, and rushed to the boulder where Jess and the children were. Mandy uttered a small cry when she saw her. Kate scooped the child into her arms. "Mandy. Mandy," was all she could say to the frightened child.

Mandy released the choke hold on Kate when the trembling finally stopped. "Is my daddy gone like my momma? The lady said she was gone for good and good riddance."

"Yes," Kate told Mandy, drying her eyes, "your daddy is gone for good." She looked to Jess for confirmation.

He nodded. "I checked him on the way down here."

Behind them, Megan reminded them of other duties. "It's time to go. The horses are getting restless. I called the sheriff and reported what happened here."

"Yes," Kate said fervently. "Let's go home."

Mandy rode with Kate while Jeremy went with his father. Exhausted by the ordeal, they made the trip down the logging road in silence, then took a shortcut through the woods. Mandy went to sleep in Kate's arms.

Two hours later they arrived at the house. Sirens had wailed along the logging road for the past hour or more. The sheriff drove up when they entered the yard at the house. After a glance at the sleeping child, he told them quietly that all that needed to be done at the moment was finished.

"Come by the office in a day or two and give your depositions," he requested. He turned to Jeremy and held out his hand. "That was a sharp bit of tracking you did. We could use a man like you. Think about law enforcement when you decide on a career."

Kate paused on the porch steps and gave Jeremy a grateful smile. "He's a true hero. He helped get Mandy out of the trailer and away while Jess took care of Collins."

Gene looked a little sheepish. "That reminds me. About fifty reporters are up there now. They'll be down here soon. I told them what happened, the way Megan here told me when she called. I, uh, also filled them in on the background."

Jess pinned a sharp gaze on the sheriff. "Just exactly what background?"

"Well, you know, like father, like son. Heroes and all. Unless I miss my guess, you'll both make the national news tonight."

Jess clenched his teeth as if he wanted to bite nails…or the sheriff. Kate, tired beyond reacting to additional information at this moment, carried Mandy inside and put the child in bed after bathing and checking her for ticks and scrapes, then she stood beside the bed and gazed at the little one with a heart overflowing with love and gratitude.

At the sound of a car, she returned downstairs. Gene had left. So had Megan. Jess and Jeremy were heading for the apartment.

"We need to shower before the deluge of the media," Jess told her with a grimace.

"And eat," Jeremy added.

She remembered the food she had packed and hadn't thought of until that moment. "Lunch first, then we'll face the reporters and get it over, okay?"

Jess nodded and walked on. She gazed after him and his son, her heart crowding her chest, making her ache.

She loved them. Jess, who guarded his heart and his dreams with all his might. Jeremy, his wonderful, smart, sensitive son. And Mandy, the gift she'd never dared hope for. She loved them. All of them.

Exhausted, she went inside to freshen up and prepare the meal. But there was no time for food for the next two hours. With notebooks and cameras in hand, reporters and TV crews arrived within minutes of the sheriff's departure.

For the next two days Kate found she rarely had time to eat as all of them were besieged with questions and demands for exclusive interviews. Seeing herself with Mandy, Jess and Jeremy on national television was like watching someone else pretending to be her.

By the third day it was over as quickly as it had begun. The rescue had become old news. Kate gave a silent prayer of thanks while she and Mandy worked in the garden Monday morning.

"Look," Kate said to Mandy. "See how the bug curls up into a little ball."

Mandy gingerly lifted the roly-poly and studied it. When it uncurled, she dropped it, startled, then she laughed. "Find another one," she ordered.

"Look under the leaves. The little devils like to hide there, then sneak out and eat holes in everything."

While Mandy searched, Kate sat back on her heels and gazed absently at Medicine Bow Peak. The growing season was nearly over. She sighed, acknowledging the emptiness inside.

Jess and Jeremy were leaving today. Their going would bore twin holes into her heart. She hadn't meant for it to happen, but there it was—her love for them, the son *and* the father.

Within her the emptiness stirred briefly, but it wasn't as cold or as bleak as it had once been. Mandy had filled part of the void, her brightness an antidote for the darkest night.

Jeremy had promised Megan he'd be back next summer to help with the horses. If she wanted him. Megan had assured the youngster she did. So had Kate when she'd invited him to visit with her as often as he could.

Jeremy had asked her to come to Houston. He'd

volunteered to show her and Mandy the local tourist attractions. Jess had been startled by the invitation.

They'd been sitting on the front porch last night when he'd told her they had to return to their home and Jeremy had delivered his impromptu invitation. Kate had caught Jess's expression and knew he'd never thought of having them visit.

The past month had been a brief but intense interlude of companionship and danger. Those things forged a bond, but it was temporary.

Tomorrow was the first of July. Time to turn over a page on the calendar of life. Once she had tried to mend every broken creature that had crossed her path. Fate had taught her it couldn't be done. Once she'd wanted to die when she lost everything dear to her. That hadn't happened, either.

Jess had his own demons to fight. Like her, he would have to learn to accept those things he couldn't change. Time made all grief easier to bear. Another lesson.

"Look!" Mandy shouted. "A butterfly."

Kate watched the child forego the search for bugs and chase the butterfly, her bare feet crushing a few plants as she raced away. It was a sign of the future. Kids stepped on their parents' hearts as they discovered their own road to happiness.

No matter. Love was worth a few heartaches.

That was something else she'd learned this past month. She would treasure the moments she'd had and let go of the rest. Jess would become part of the good memories.

Mandy returned to her side and rested as they watched the butterfly lift and float away on the breeze.

Kate smiled even as she felt the sweet weight of Mandy's complete trust. A child's love was a gift. A responsibility. A joy.

She stood and took the child's hand. "Come. It'll soon be time for you to go visit Aunt Megan while I sign some papers in town."

Together they went up the path to the house.

Jess handed his suitcase to his son. The boy dashed out of the apartment and down the stairs like a young gazelle. Jess smiled wryly. Those days were long past for him.

On the trip back to the house, each movement of his knee resulting in needles of agony, he'd accepted the fate he couldn't change. At forty-one, a man had to bow gracefully to the ravages of time. Younger men would have to do the exciting chase scenes and drug busts and arrests. Older guys such as him handled the paperwork.

Time for plan B. Law school.

Giving a sardonic snort of laughter, he glanced around one last time. The apartment was neat and clean. Kate wouldn't have to do any work. He sighed, placed the key on the hook by the phone and went down the stairs.

He was also giving up on solving Bunny's case. He'd run into a dead end on every front. As Kate had said, there came a time when the past had to be put in its place and a person had to move on. He had reached that point.

"Jeremy! Jess!" Mandy yelled. She came flying out the door and over to the pickup. "Here, I broughted you some brownies."

"I brought you some brownies," Jeremy corrected.

"No. *I* broughted them to *you*," she insisted.

Jeremy gave up the grammar lesson. "Thanks. These will be great on the road."

She handed the boy the package and threw her arms around his neck in a stranglehold of affection.

A knot formed in Jess's throat for no good reason. He looked away, only to encounter eyes so blue they mesmerized a man. He swallowed hard before speaking. "It's time to be off."

"So it is," Kate agreed. Her face was calm, her smile wide and friendly and genuine.

A flicker of irritation grated over his nerves. But then, what had he expected her to do—throw herself sobbing into his arms and beg him to stay?

Ha. Not his Katie.

His Katie? Hardly.

Forcing the futile thoughts at bay, he took her hand, leaned forward and planted one last kiss on her soft lips. She lightly touched his shoulder, then drew away. He wasn't nearly satisfied with the chaste touch. With Kate he would always crave her sweet caresses and little moans of delight and...too much.

She made him dream, this woman. And that only ended in pain. Except for the moments in her arms. His body set up a clamor as he recalled those moments. They had been too few; this parting was taking too many.

"I'm ready," Jeremy said in a new, older manner that still startled Jess. The boy had grown over the summer. He didn't want to leave, but he'd accepted that they had to.

Washed up. Jess grimaced. The words no longer

filled him with bitterness, but they were true, none-theless. Besides, he'd never been very good at having a family. It wasn't in the cards for him. Never had been. Never would be.

Kate lifted Mandy. The two females waved good-bye when Jess drove down the driveway. At the county road he glanced over at his son. Green eyes the same color as his—like looking into his own soul—gazed back at him with stoic regard.

This summer had been idyllic in many ways, but their real lives were in Texas. Fishing, boating, chasing a bad guy, those had been fun, or at least exciting, but not real.

Jess clenched his teeth at the lurch in his own heart. Making love with Kate had been real, but it had been a summer thing, full of promise, but he'd encountered promises before.

Life was filled with illusions. Being together. Making love. Sharing danger and worry as they searched for the kids and the armed madman. Knowing the joy and relief of finding Jeremy and Mandy alive and unharmed. Yeah, they had forged a bond. But nothing was forever.

He waved to the sheriff when he stopped in town to sign the typed deposition. When Kate and Megan had also signed their statements, the case would be closed. Except for Kate's adoption of Mandy. That was already in the works.

Gene had indicated the powers that be had thought Jess would be a good addition to their law enforce-ment staff. Nice to be wanted, but he really was con-sidering law school.

Thinking of the paperwork, he grimaced. Lawyers

didn't *solve* cases; they argued them. Heading for the city hall, he told Jeremy to meet him at the café for lunch in thirty minutes and gave him some quarters for the video arcade.

"Dad?"

"Yeah?"

The youngster bounded out of the truck. "I wish…"

Jess waited, knowing what was coming.

"I wish we could stay. Like, for always."

"Live there, you mean?" It was a possibility that had kept intruding in his thoughts the past three days, no matter how many arguments he mustered against the idea.

"Yeah. We could go home, pack up and move here. The apartment is empty at Kate's place."

Jess swallowed hard, sudden longing filling his chest to painful tightness. A dream, that's what it was, one too fragile to hold. And one he wanted with everything in him.

Kate. He wanted *her*. In every way a man could.

"Sounds as if you've been doing some checking," he said, stalling for time as he tried to regain an emotional distance. He knew about dreams. He didn't want his son to be hurt by wanting too much.

"I talked to Shannon," the youngster admitted. "She says you have a job here. If you want it."

"I was thinking of law school." He heard the desperate determination in his own voice.

"Oh." Jeremy kept his tone neutral.

Jess carefully explained why they shouldn't make a spur-of-the-moment decision—that Jeremy needed to be with his friends again, return to his old school and see if he really wanted to leave the city and its many activities for the back country.

"Wind River is a long way from all you've ever known," he concluded, feeling wise and parental while loneliness and hunger ate at him. From far away he heard the caw of crows.

A warning…

Instead of growing sullen and argumentative as he once would have, Jeremy nodded solemnly.

Jess's heart shot to his throat. Yeah, his son had grown up a lot. He wished he could give the boy everything he wanted—a happy family, a home where love dwelt.

You can, some part of him said. A picture of a ranch house, old-fashioned and secure on its foundations leaped into his inner vision. Kate was there. He pictured her smile that could warm a man clear through. The hunger churned within. It wasn't only physical.

"Shannon said with your experience at solving cases and all, you could conduct all their criminal investigations," Jeremy told him earnestly. "And there's a branch of the state university within driving distance. Shannon is taking classes there, psychology or something. She said you two could car pool if you wanted."

"Oh, she did, did she?" Jess said wryly, feeling the not-too-subtle pressure from his son. There was a problem the boy hadn't thought of. Kate might not want him as a permanent fixture in her life. Like him, she'd tried marriage, and look what it had gotten her.

Again he felt the pull of her, the womanliness, the heat of their passion, the goodness of her nature. Because of her, he could feel the lure of the land and the community, like roots growing right out of his feet into the rocky soil.

Need rushed through him, so great he trembled. He had slept with her, awakened beside her, prepared meals, worried, laughed and made love with her. In one month they had shared more than most couples did in a lifetime.

Staring at the mountains, their lofty peaks softly caressed by clouds, he experienced a lifting and lightening. Loneliness, he realized, was a heavy load.

Smiling ruefully, he wondered why he had ever thought he could leave. He wasn't even very shocked at the revelation. However, it was a leap of faith, hoping that Kate would want him, that they could make a go of it as a family.

Dreams. They were scary things.

Jeremy sighed and gazed at the ground. "You probably wouldn't like living here. It gets a lot of snow in winter. And working with small-town cops might be a hassle."

"Why don't we try it and see?" Jess suggested and realized the words had been there, inside him, for days, maybe years, just waiting for the right place to grow and spring forth.

Jeremy's head shot up, his eyes alight with surprise. "Wh-what? You mean…like, we'll move here? Really?"

"We'll keep the apartment in Houston," Jess decided, thinking quickly. "If by Christmas break we decide Wind River is our kind of place, we'll get our things and move out permanently. If not, we'll go home. Back to Houston."

That should give him and Kate enough time to sort it all out. He tried not to think about a sane female's reaction to a proposal from a crippled cop. Then his heart reminded him Kate wasn't like that. But he didn't want pity, either.

"Neat! Can I call Kate and Mandy and tell them now? There's a pay phone at the drug store."

Jess took the coward's way out. "Sure. Tell Kate we want the apartment until Christmas for sure."

"You'll tell them?" Jeremy asked, gesturing toward the building that house both county and town functions. "After you sign the deposition and everything, you'll tell Shannon and the sheriff you'll take the job?"

"Sure."

That part was easy. Kate was a different matter. Jess had no idea what he would say when he saw her. He realized he was nervous—a hard thing for a cop to admit. Reaching for a dream might be a fool's task. It was a chance he'd have to take. He didn't let himself think beyond that.

"So, what's happening out your way?" Shannon inquired.

Kate and her cousin had gone to lunch after Kate had signed the papers. Jess, she'd learned, had been in and left the courthouse shortly before she'd arrived. He and his son were on their way home, to their real home, she amended, glad that things seemed to be working out for them.

"Nothing," she said. "Jess and Jeremy are gone. The apartment is empty. I don't think I'll rent it this year."

Shannon nodded, then glanced at her watch. "Got to run. I'm in court this afternoon." She wrinkled her nose.

Kate watched her cousin leave the restaurant to return to her office, then she simply sat and watched the flow of traffic and residents along the main street.

With a child to support, she had decided she needed to increase her income. Rory Daniels had told several businessmen about the system she'd installed for him and how she'd personalized it. Now several people wanted their computers updated and "fixed" to reflect their business needs.

That very morning she'd agreed to take over the accounting and set up bookkeeping systems on computers for three local business owners. She had three more waiting until she could work them in. She was going to be very busy until well after tax time in April.

Everything was going great. So why did she feel so down in the dumps?

The answer appeared across the street. She blinked in surprise. Jess came out of the sheriff's office. He and Gene were talking like bosom buddies. She wondered why he wasn't on the road for Houston.

She touched her lips, which felt as lonely as the rest of her. She frowned, then sighed, then smiled. Time had a way of making things better. Meanwhile she and Mandy would be quite happy without any men in their lives, other than as casual friends.

The waitress brought the check. She paid and left the diner. Jess and the sheriff had both disappeared. Standing on the sidewalk, she fished her list of chores out of her purse and perused it. The hardware store first, she decided, then the grocery. Megan had Mandy with her for another riding lesson, then would put the child down for an afternoon nap, so she needn't hurry.

She took a deep breath of crystalline air. After the rain last night, the sky had cleared, the temperature had warmed and the afternoon was one of those beautiful moments that brought an ache to a person's heart.

"Hello, Kate," a masculine voice said.

Kate turned and stared into eyes that were dark green, sort of mysterious and moody, maybe a bit hesitant, but she also saw control, composure and a sly bit of humor there.

Her insides went to jelly as the familiar fire blazed into being inside her. She resisted the urge to touch him. While she nodded and smiled warily, her heart leaped around in her chest before settling to a hard pounding.

The look in those fierce eyes, when she met his gaze, caused her to shake. They were telling her things...or was she imagining it?

"I need to talk to you. Let's go home," he suggested, his voice husky but oddly gentle. "I'll follow you."

Suddenly she wasn't sure of her control. If they were alone... If he touched her... She glance around in desperation. "Where's Jeremy?"

"He's visiting with Shannon until I call and tell them it's okay."

That seemed odd. At his urging she went to her car. They drove back to her house, him behind her all the way. "I forgot the groceries," she said when they entered the kitchen.

"You can get them later. After we talk."

She sat down abruptly and clasped her hands on the place mats. "What shall we talk about?"

He pulled a chair close to hers. "Us," he suggested on a somewhat wry note. His smile was solemn when she glanced at him.

Then she couldn't look away. It was as if something in his eyes had fused with something in her. They gazed at each other, messages flying with the speed of light between them. A shiver raced over her, leaving behind a trail of chill bumps. He noticed and rubbed her arms until they disappeared.

"I meant to wait until things were settled, but I can't hold out another minute."

"You're not making a lot of sense, Detective," she said, not letting herself hope or dream or do anything foolish. Because she'd learned better. Inside, the trembling increased. Because she was hoping and dreaming...and she wanted very much to kiss him.

"I'm the new chief of investigations for the sheriff's department, pending final approval by the county commissioners. Since they approved the position knowing I was the sheriff's first choice, I think I'm a shoo-in, don't you?"

She blinked and tried to make sense of this. "Well, yes. I guess."

"You're not going to make this easy," he murmured. "Kate Mulholland, reclusive widow that you are, do you think you could stand having a gimpy-legged cop and his son around, like, permanently?"

His deprecating humor caught her off guard. Her heart beat crazily. She stared at him.

"We're too good together to ignore it all," he said, as if it were as simple as that.

"Ignore what?" She felt as if she'd missed part of the conversation.

"Would you take me for a husband, lover, friend for life?" he requested in a tone that sent the blood surging wildly through her body.

She opened her mouth, but nothing came out.

"Let's get married, Kate. Our kids need stability, someone to believe in. They need us," he said.

She heard, *I need someone to believe in, someone who believes in me.*

"You must know I'm crazy about you. You're everything I ever dreamed of in a woman. You and Mandy and Jeremy…me…we'll make a good family for each other," he said, looking a bit anxious himself.

She heard, *I love you. I love our kids. I want us to be a family together.*

"Yes," she agreed softly, those irrepressible dreams springing up anew. If she was dreaming, she hoped she didn't wake soon. "I think I've loved you since…since…"

He pulled her to her feet and into his arms. "Yeah, from the very first day we met and I rescued you from that dangerous water hose gone berserk."

She felt his chuckle against her breasts. She smiled, too, knowing humor was easier for him to handle as they faced their feelings. Then, for no reason and for all the reasons in the world, they laughed at the absurdity of it all. Then they simply looked their fill of each other for several seconds.

"I couldn't have left. I'd have missed you all my life," he said, suddenly somber.

She heard more than the words. There was the need and the hunger. More than those, there was the promise of sharing life and making a home for their two children. For a second she thought of the past and felt a tiny chill of fear.

"You'll be able to continue your investigation," she reminded him.

"No," he said firmly. "You were right. The past belongs to the past. I want a future. With you. Only you."

His words were his promise, his pledge to her for all time. Tears knotted in her throat and she could only nod. Needing his touch, she held out her hand.

When he took it, she turned and walked up the stairs with her love. In tender passion and earnest words, she pledged her faith and love. He promised his whole, long, loving future to her and their family.

"Get up! Get up, everybody! Santa was here!"

Jess opened his eyes at Mandy's excited news and glanced at the clock. "Five," he murmured.

Kate moaned. They had been up until all hours putting together the toy kitchen Mandy had her heart set upon. Jess and Jeremy had put the stove, sink and refrigerator together while she read the instructions and kept them supplied with cookies and hot chocolate. They had had to shush each other often as their laughter threatened to get out of hand at the complicated task. It was past midnight before they finished.

"Mommy! Daddy! Jeremy!" Mandy yelled into the bedrooms.

"I'm coming," Jeremy grumbled from down the hall.

"Let's get up," Jess said, kissing her ear. "One, two, three…"

They flung back the covers. She grabbed a robe while he pulled on sweats. They washed up and headed downstairs. Jeremy was tickling Mandy, entertaining her until the adults arrived.

"Look at all the stuff!" Mandy yelled.

"Wow, that kitchen looks just like our big one," Kate said. "Maybe you'd better open this present from Jeremy first."

Jeremy handed the girl a package. Mandy shrieked when she saw the pots and pans that went with her kitchen. After that, they took turns opening gifts until the living room was a sea of crumpled paper and boxes spilling over with new treasures.

Kate rubbed her cheek over the soft sweater set from Jess. The color matched her eyes.

"Here's something to go with that," he said, and pulled a box from under the sofa.

She found a string of pearls inside when she opened it. She looked at him with her heart in her eyes. "They're beautiful."

"They're nice," he corrected. "You're beautiful." He pulled her close.

"Are you two going to start kissing?" Mandy demanded.

"Let's go fix breakfast, roly-poly, and give them some lip-hanging time," Jeremy suggested.

Jess grimaced while the two kids went into the

kitchen, Mandy arguing she wasn't a bug. ''Lip-hanging?''

''It's the act that counts,'' Kate said, laughing.

''Yeah.''

He kissed her then. Or she kissed him. It worked both ways, love did. He'd learned that during the three short months of their marriage. When both loved and gave, not always equally but in whatever amount was needed at the moment, it all evened out.

The kiss was long and mutually satisfying, a promise of things to come when they were alone and a reminder of all they shared. He felt the sensual hum of anticipation swirl through his blood. He could wait for night and their moments alone.

''I have something for you,'' she murmured. She brought a package out of the closet and handed it to him.

He gave her an amused but wary perusal, then tore the paper off. The gift was a tiny statue of a space soldier. Hero of the Universe was the legend engraved on the base.

''To my very own hero,'' she whispered.

Jess managed a grin, but inside he was feeling all the tenderness she induced in him. He traced her lips with one finger, glad that he'd stopped here on his way to nowhere. Here he'd found what he'd looked for all his life—his own little ragtag family made up of a cop with a bummed-out knee, an idealistic ten-year-old, a widow with her own hidden scars and an orphan who had lived through more than most adults in her short life. He wouldn't trade one of them for the world.

Kate pressed a hand over her abdomen which had

once felt barren. Now she was filled with life, rich with all the pleasures love could bestow.

"I love you," he said.

He put an arm around her, his eyes going dark as he pulled her close. That wildly intense awareness bloomed between them, the same as it had from the first. They smiled the way lovers do, then walked slowly toward the kitchen where the children laughed and argued over the breakfast menu.

"Two wounded soldiers," Jess murmured, pausing at the doorway. "It was a miracle we found each other, but we did."

They gazed at each other in complete understanding.

"We did," Jess repeated, all the joy of Christmas in his gentle laughter.

Jeremy and Mandy paused, then, seeing their parents laughing, they did, too.

To Kate it was the happiest sound, flowing to the farthest corners of her soul, all its empty spaces now filled. It was a good feeling.

* * * * *

Look out for Laurie Paige's next instalment of
THE WINDRAVEN LEGACY *with*
When I See Your Face, *available in July 2002.*

▼™ SILHOUETTE®
SPECIAL EDITION™

AVAILABLE FROM 21ST JUNE 2002

DADDY IN DEMAND Muriel Jensen

That's My Baby!

When Dori McKeon found an abandoned baby she turned to estranged husband Sal Dominguez. Sal was happy to help solve the puzzle—and to try and win Dori back…this time—forever!

THE STRANGER IN ROOM 205 Gina Wilkins

Hot Off the Press

Instinct told newspaper owner Serena Schaffer that the injured man she'd found was not who he proclaimed to be. But one look into Sam's eyes and Serena was ready to believe anything…

WHEN I SEE YOUR FACE Laurie Paige

Windraven Legacy

Rory Daniels knew that if temporarily blinded Shannon Bannock could just find the courage to trust him, he could show her so much—he could show her forever…

STORMING WHITEHORN Christine Scott

Montana Brides

Storm Hunter had coldly refused Jasmine's charms. The chasm between their ages and cultures was too wide. But how could Storm continue to resist when the virginal beauty still looked at him that way?

STARTING WITH A KISS Barbara McMahon

When prim-and-proper Abigail Trent asked Dr Greg Hastings to help turn her into an irresistible temptress, she never thought that after just one kiss she would start to hope that Greg was her Prince Charming…

STRANGER IN A SMALL TOWN Ann Roth

B&B owner and single mum Alison O'Hara was like no woman loner Clint had ever met. Could she transform him into a husband—and a daddy to her little girl?

0602/23a

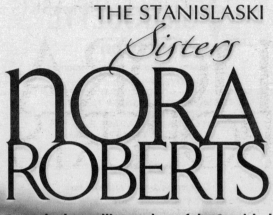

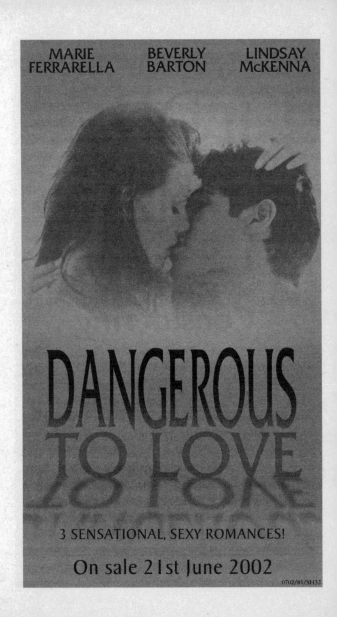

SILHOUETTE®

DESIRE™

is proud to present

Maureen Child's

BACHELOR
BATTALION

*Defending their country is their duty;
love and marriage are their rewards!*

PRINCE CHARMING IN DRESS BLUES
(*in* Special Delivery)

HIS BABY!
(*in* Secret Child)

LAST VIRGIN IN CALIFORNIA
(*in* Up Close and Passionate)

0502/SH/LC31

FREE

2 BOOKS
AND A SURPRISE GIFT!

We would like to take this opportunity to thank you for reading this Silhouette® book by offering you the chance to take TWO more specially selected titles from the Special Edition™ series absolutely FREE! We're also making this offer to introduce you to the benefits of the Reader Service™—

    ★ FREE home delivery   ★ FREE gifts and competitions
    ★ FREE monthly Newsletter   ★ Exclusive Reader Service discount
              ★ Books available before they're in the shops

Accepting these FREE books and gift places you under no obligation to buy; you may cancel at any time, even after receiving your free shipment. Simply complete your details below and return the entire page to the address below. *You don't even need a stamp!*

YES! Please send me 2 free Special Edition books and a surprise gift. I understand that unless you hear from me, I will receive 4 superb new titles every month for just £2.85 each, postage and packing free. I am under no obligation to purchase any books and may cancel my subscription at any time. The free books and gift will be mine to keep in any case.

E2ZEC

Ms/Mrs/Miss/Mr ....Initials..
BLOCK CAPITALS PLEASE

Surname...

Address...

....

....Postcode ....

Send this whole page to:
UK: FREEPOST CN81, Croydon, CR9 3WZ
EIRE: PO Box 4546, Kilcock, County Kildare (stamp required)

Offer valid in UK and Eire only and not available to current Reader Service subscribers to this series. We reserve the right to refuse an application and applicants must be aged 18 years or over. Only one application per household. Terms and prices subject to change without notice. Offer expires 30th September 2002. As a result of this application, you may receive offers from other carefully selected companies. If you would prefer not to share in this opportunity please write to The Data Manager at the address above.

Silhouette® is a registered trademark used under licence.
Special Edition™ is being used as a trademark.